A Collection of Lives

by

Martin Harris

Book 1

When the Snow Falls

approx. 17040 words

Book 2

The Sphere of

Eternal Life

approx. 18090 words

Book 3

Dark Hunger

approx. 24000 words

Book 1

When The Snow Falls

Chapter 1

Suzan stared into the hospital room where her mother lay and turning to the footsteps approaching.

" Doctor, how long before it's over?" she questioned.
" Well, it's hard to say, it could be tomorrow, or next week, or even six months," replied Doctor Hardings.
" Look at them," Suzan said looking back at the children, " they think she's just got a cold."
" You haven't told them?"
" I haven't found the right time yet." Suzan said as she stepped closer to the door.

" Mummy can I get drink?" Jenny asked her mother.
" Sure sweety." She said looking down as she stroked her daughter's hair. Jenny then hopped and skipped down the hospital hall to the water fountain. " I'd better leave you now I've got some rounds to do," the doctor said to Suzan as he placed his hand to her shoulder. " Thank you, for everything." Suzan smiled to the doctor held her head up high and entered her mother's hospital room.

" You were talking about me again weren't you." Suzan's mother asked as she raised an eyebrow. " No, not really." Suzan said taking hold of her mother's hand. " I may be old but I'm not deaf," said Estell. " You're not old grandma," Billy said as he climbed upon the bed.
" Thank you dear." Estelle reaching out to touch Billy's cheek. " So how much did you hear." Suzan taking a breath and look to her mother hoping she didn't hear too much. " Enough to know I've got up to six months."

Where are you going in six months grandma?" Jenny
questioned as she came back into the room. " Far away
dear, sort of like a holiday," Estelle trying to explain.
Billy looking puzzled asked " Will you be coming back?"
" No dear." Estelle looked to Suzan and gave a half smile.
" Can we come visit you?" Jenny asked leaning onto the
bed. " No dear, where I'm going it's just too far away."
Estelle explained as she held onto her granddaughter's
hand. " Come on you two it's time to go home and
grandma need her rest." Suzan collected their things and
kissed her mother on the cheek, Billy leaned forward,
and he too kissed his grandmother on the cheek. " Do we
have to go; can't we stay just a little longer." Jenny asked
with big puppy dog eyes and pushing her bottom lip out.
" Honey, grandma needs her sleep if you want her to get
better." Jenny shrugged her shoulders and gave Estelle a
kiss and all three wished her a goodnight.

Estelle lay there in total silence and the room partly lit
by moonlight thinking of years past. Thinking of when
she was a young woman just turning twenty and the one,
she loved. Her eyes grew heavy and with a smile she
slowly drifted off to sleep.

" Isn't it beautiful." Estelle said holding John's hand
looking over a field of wild blossoms. " Come on then.
"John said looking at Estelle. " What?" Estelle was
puzzled. " Let's run through them like we did when we
were young." " Alright, I'll race you to the other side."
Estelle said as she began to run gaining a head start. "
Hey, wait up." John yelled. " For the counties best
runner, you sure are slow." Estelle hollered from halfway
across the field. Butterflies danced on the breeze as both
John and Estelle ran through the hundreds of wild
purple flowers and with all the butterflies it was a sight

to be there was as many butterflies as there were flowers. Not looking where she was running Estelle tripped and fell at the same time letting out a scream. John stopped in his tracks looked around and then started running again. " Estelle; Estelle, where are you? "John frantically called. There was no answer, he kept running in the same direction as Estelle, and then he found her, she lay there motionless. John's eyes widened with fear, he took a deep breath and knelt beside her. He gently rolled Estelle onto her back and wiped the dirt away from her face. As John looked up for any sign of help Estelle opened one of her eyes to see if he was looking, when she saw he wasn't she opened the other eye and said, " Gotcha," and then began to laugh. In shock John dropped Estelle back into the dirt and stood up. " What the hell do you think you're doing," he bellowed. " There's no need to start cussing, I was only having a bit of fun." Estelle said while lying there in the dirt. " Grow up," John said as he began to walk away. " John wait," Estelle yelled as she got off the ground. But John paid no attention and kept on walking. Estelle picked up a clump of grass and dirt and threw it hitting John in the back. He let out a bit of a yell and fell to the ground moaning. Estelle gasped for air and ran to John as fast as she could. " John I'm sorry," she yelled out as she reached him. He then turned over and started laughing. " Gotcha back," he said still laughing. He then sat up and kissed Estelle on her soiled cheek. " John please, someone may be watching." Estelle pulled back and looked around. " We better get back or your father will be having fits."

John took Estelle's hand and they walked to the edge of the field to the beginning of the track. " Wait I want to get one last look at the field," Estelle said turning back to take in the beauty of the flowers. " It's beautiful isn't it," he said placing his arm around her shoulder. " It's a shame it it'll be gone when the snow falls." Estelle said as they looked across the rainbow-coloured field.

As the dream went out of focus another voice entered. " Estelle, Estelle." The voice echoed. Estelle's eyes crept open and with the sharp sunlight cutting through the window she could see a man standing beside the bed. " John," she whispered. " Estelle it's me, Doctor Harding," he said as he wiped a tear from her cheek. " Yes, of course." Estell said as she looked away. " I'm here to give you a check over," he said as he went over her chart to study the overnight ob.'s. " Well am I still going to die?" she asked looking out the window. " Estelle you're doing just fine," he answered, " the nurse will be in shortly to bath you." " Do you know when my daughter is coming back?" " I'm sure she'll be in around lunch time." He replied. The doctor left the room and left Estelle in her bed with a book. She felt so alone and longed to see her field of flowers that she once knew as a young girl. Time slowly crept on as she eagerly waited for her family to visit. Tired from waiting she slowly drifted back to sleep and once again began to dream of the beauty of spring breaking through winter.

" Estelle honey," mother called, " When you've finished your chores you can take some fresh bread to Mrs Peters." " Mother is it ok if I go over to John's house for a while," Estelle asked trying to look as cute as possible. " Well; " her mother paused, " ok only if you're back by supper. " Don't worry I will," Estelle grabbed the loaf of bread and hopped and skipped out of the back door and down the garden path. Along the way she passed the field of wildflowers that grew nearby. Estelle loved to stop and smell the wonderful aromas that would float on the summer breezes and see all the flowers sway like they were dancing, and the butterflies and bees that would hop from flower to flower, this always brought a smile to her face even when she was feeling down. Estelle gathered herself and continued on her way.

" Hello Mrs Peters, it's me Estelle." She waited for a moment and then ran around to the back of the house and called again. " Hello Mrs Peters, I've brought some bread." " Over here dear." A voice came from behind the garden shed. " I'm in the strawberry patch." Estelle looked around and skipped down the path to the garden where Mrs Peters was waiting. " And how are you today, Estelle?" " Just dandy Mrs peters." Estelle replied looking hungrily at the strawberries. " Mm the bread smells so good your mother really does a wonderful job; would you like a piece." " Oh, I couldn't, I've just eaten. But I could possibly squeeze in a strawberry though." Estelle said with her eyes still fixed on the patch. " Very well dear, help yourself." Estelle licked her lips and began to eat. " Try not to eat too many dear you might get a tummy ache." Warned Mrs Peters. " Don't worry I won't I'll just have three." " I'm going inside now so I'll see you later and please thank your mother for me," Mrs Peters said as she hobbled out of the garden. Estelle ate three big red juicy strawberries and then picked two extra for John. She knew Mrs Peters wouldn't mind as she knew Estelle would always take the two extras.

" Grandma, grandma, are you sleeping?" Jenny as she leaned over the edge of the hospital bed. " Jenny be quiet you'll wake the whole hospital," Billy said trying to pull his sister from the bed. " Come on you two sit on the chair and wait till grandma wakes up." Suzan took both children by the hand and sat them on the large armchair next to the bed. " Suzan are you there?" Estelle whispered as she slowly opened her eyes. " Yes mum." " Could you please help me sit up I can't see the children." Estelle asked as she struggled with the bed covers. Suzan motioned to the children, " Billy go to the other side and straighten the pillows while I hold grandma." " That's better, thank you dear." Estelle smiled to billy then gently touched him on the head for the kind gesture. " Now come and sit on the bed and tell me what you've both been up to."

" Yesterday when we got home, we had chocolate sundaes," Jenny explaining as her eyes lit up, " grandma did you have chocolate sundaes when you were a little girl?" " Oh yes dear all the time, we even had fresh strawberries on top and sometimes sprinkled with nuts." " Now would you two like me to get you something from the canteen?" Suzan asked as she picked up her purse. " Oh yes please can I have an ice cream," Jenny asked. " And can I have a milkshake?" Billy added. " Sure. Would you like something mum?" " No thank you dear, I have everything I want right here," Estelle said looking at both the children. " Ok then I won't be long." Suzan then turned and left the room.

" Grandma, how much longer are you going to be in here?" Jenny asked as she lay beside Estelle. " Not much longer, the doctors are doing everything they can, so I can leave soon."
" I don't like hospitals much, they smell funny and there's always sick people." Billy said as he looked around the room. " Why are you sick grandma?" Jenny asked as she sat up. " Well Jenny, I'm very old, and when

you get old you get sicker much quicker," she explained as she stroked Jenny's hair.

" Here we go," Suzan entered the room, " Here's your milkshake and Jenny here's your ice cream." " Ooo thank you mummy," Jenny said with a grin that spread from ear to ear. " Thanks mum," Billy said, " would you like some grandma?" " Not this time dear, you have it." " Grandma, tell us about when you were a little girl," asking Jenny as she climbed onto the bed. " Yes, please gran." Billy then too climbed onto the bed. " Very well." Estelle began to make herself comfortable. " Mum, are you sure," Suzan touched her mother's hand. " I'm Sure. Now let me see:" Estelle began to set the scene and continued where her dream had ended.

After picking the strawberries for John Estelle placed them carefully in her pocket and quickly made her way to a small dirt track that led to john's house. The day was beautiful, the sky a deep blue and not a cloud to be seen. Birds could be heard in the surrounding trees and the scent of honeysuckle drifted on the breeze. As Estelle skipped into John's front yard, she took one last deep breath of the honeysuckle filled air before entering the house. " John," Estelle hollered as she knocked on the front door, " are you home? I have strawberries." Estelle could hear footsteps coming towards the front door, so she took a few steps back. " Who is there?" a voice questioned from the other side of the door. " It's me, Estelle. Is John home? I have strawberries for him from Mrs Peters, and mum said I can play for a while." The front door opened, and John's mother Mrs Cavanagh stood there. " He's up in his room Estelle go right up." " Thank you, Mrs Cavanaugh." Estelle said with a bit of trouble and handed her a strawberry. Estelle dashed through the door and shot up the stairway to John's door. Without making a noise she crept into his room and gently placed her hands over his eyes. " Guess who?" She said trying her best to make her voice deeper.

" Hi Estelle," John said with a chuckle. " How did you know it was me," she said giving him a stern look placing her hands on her hips. " Well, your hands are too small to be my dad's and your voice sounds nothing like my mother's," he explained. " Well, I have some strawberries from Mrs Peters for you." Estelle pulled out the remainder of the strawberries from her pocket and presented them in her hand; John eyes grew bigger and in a moment's glance he ate them like it was the first time he had ever been fed.

The two children wondered down to the creek that lay at the bottom of John's parent's property to try and catch some tadpoles and frogs. Estelle wasn't a girlish type of girl, was more at home in the mud chasing frogs and lizards. Some hours had passed since they at the creek and with endless frogs and other creatures they hadn't noticed the time fly by.

" John, quick I've got one," Estelle shouted with joy. " Hold onto it," John yelled as he ran through the ankle-deep mud. " Hurry John there's another one." John ran a little faster to try and catch up with the other frog that was trying desperately to escape their clutches. Without warning John lost his step, tripping and falling face first into the mud, sliding up to Estelle's feet. She laughed so hard she had dropped the frog and fell back into the mud; John sat to his knees and began laughing back. Estelle grabbed a fist full of mud and threw it as though she was throwing a baseball hitting John in the face knocking him on his back, the air was silent, only the sound of frogs jumping in the mud could be heard, then suddenly both children burst into laughter.

" Come on it's getting late, mother will be wondering where I am," Estelle said as she helped John out of the mud. The two children parted ways at the edge of the creek and started their walk home. Estelle desperately trying to scrape off the mud before she reached her destination.

Chapter 2

" Ok you two it's time to go home," Suzan announced. " Do we have to?" Jenny asked as she held onto her grandmother's hand. " Yes, we do, grandma needs her sleep, or did you forget that grandma is sick. Suzan continued collection her children's things.

Once again Estelle was left alone, not just from her family but from the one she loved as a youth. She began to weep and remember her life and how she wished it could all start again. Something was wrong, Estelle's vision grew blurred, her breathing light, she struggled for her next breath, a slight panic filled her mind she felt her time was near. She reached out for the pager that lay on the bedside table and with what little strength she had she tightly squeezed the pager and the everything went black.

Alarms sounded in her room echoing down the hospital hall. " Doctor hurry there's a code blue in room two eleven," a nurse responded. " Hurry it's Mrs Cavanagh's room. Get me a heart and lung monitor and set up the oxygen tent," instructed Doctor Harding's, " Nurse Collins call Mrs Cavanagh's daughter!" A medical team of doctors and nursed rushed to Estelle's room.

With children dragging behind her, Suzan came running into the hospital, making their way through the corridors that lead to her mother's room. " Doctor, how is she? what's happened?" Suzan questioned her voice full of fear. " It seems she had a mild heart attack and one of her lungs had stopped working," he explained as he placed a hand on Suzan's shoulder, " Your mother is doing much better now but still has a lot of recovery. As you can see, we have place her in an oxygen tent to help purify the air around her." " Is it ok for me to see her?" she asked trying to hold back tears from the children. " Of course, it is, but it might be best if the children stay in the waiting room as all this can be too much all at once for them." " Yes of course." Suzan turned to the children and gave them huge hugs, " Billy, Jenny, I'm going to see grandma now so will you wait here for me, please."   " Why can't we see grandma mummy?" Jenny quietly asked. " Well honey, grandma is really sick, and the doctor thinks it's better that mummy should visit so we don't tire grandma out too much, ok." She carefully explained to the children.

Suzan gradually approached her mother's room stopping at the door to wipe away any tears that may have settled on her cheek. She took a deep breath and entered the room. " Oh mum," Suzan whispered as she took Estelle's hand. " I love you mum." A tear began to roll down her cheek as she gazed upon her mother, she studied the lines on her face that were softly lit by the dim hospital light above the bed and felt the gratitude of having such an amazing person for her mother.

Morning came, and Suzan had fallen asleep, still holding onto her mother's hand. As the sunlight crept into the room Suzan's eyes opened, she looked to her mother and saw she was still sleeping, so she straightened herself at the same time rubbing the stiffness that settled in her neck. Lifting her weary body, she walked over to the window to view the day that was ahead.

" You're blocking the sunlight." Suzan's eyes widened. " Mum!" She gasped turning to Estelle. " Would you please get out of the light," Estelle asked impatiently. " Can you get the doctor I want this blasted off." Suzan ran out the room and down the corridor to the nurse's station. " Doctor Hardings, it's mum she's awake and I think she's ok, she's wanting the mask off." Suzan said laughing and crying all at the same time. The Doctor, two nurses came to Estelle's room to begin some tests and Suzan hurried down the hall to the waiting room where the two children slept. " Jenny, Billy," Suzan gently stroked their heads to wake them, " grandmas awake."

" Good morning Estelle and how are you feeling." Asked Doctor Hardings as he began to examine her. " Well, it's about time," Estelle said as everyone came through the door. The doctor continued to examine her as she looked around at the nurses. " Well, did you find anything," she questioned raising an eyebrow. " It's amazing, everything is back to normal." Hardings said standing back rubbing his chin. Suzan came into the room but standing back to give the nurse's room to do their job. " Could I see you outside for a moment Suzan?" " Sure," she answered with a puzzled look. Suzan and Doctor Hardings wandered down the corridor till they almost reached the waiting room.

" I don't know what it is but, it's like there's something pulling her through," the Doctor said with a puzzling voice, " from the turn she had last night your mother should not be awake today, it's like she's holding on for something. Suzan, do you know of anything, or anyone that she could be wanting?" Suzan thought for a moment and then something came to her. " Mum used to talk of a place she used to go as a young girl and where she used to go with my father, maybe that's it. I know she is always talking about this field of flowers she played in." Suzan explained. " Is it far to these flowers?" " Well flying it's at least three hours and driving maybe an overnight tip to Driftwood Valley and winter is only a few weeks away." " What happens in winter?" Hardings questioned. " Snow, Doctor. The valley gets covered in it and nothing grows back for months and I'm afraid it could be too late by then." Suzan said with a sound of despair in her voice. " We can only do our best to make her as comfortable as possible," said the doctor as he took Suzan by the hand.

" Mummy can we see grandma now?" Jenny asked as she took hold of her mother's other hand. " Soon my darlings, we'll go in after lunch." " Why can't we see her now?" Billy questioned. " Well, grandma got very sick last night, and she needs a lot of sleep to get better," Suzan explained.

Suzan and the children arrived back at the hospital fresh and ready to see Estelle, Jenny holding tightly onto a bunch of flowers skipping towards her grandmother's room. She stopped at the door and peeked in. " Come in dear," Estelle said as she looked towards the door. Jenny entered the room trying to hide the flowers behind her. " Where's your mother and Billy?" " Oh, they should be here soon, I ran ahead of them, so I could see you first." Jenny pulled out the flowers from behind her and presented then to Estelle and placed a kiss on her cheek. " Jenny, there you are," Suzan said entering the room, " I've told you before never to run in the hospital." " I didn't run mummy, I skipped." Jenny gave a grin. " How are you mum?" Suzan asked as she leaned to give Estelle a kiss. " Much better thank you dear." " Grandma, can you tell us another story from when you were a little girl?" Billy asked climbing onto the bed. " Could you get me some water please?" Estelle looked to Suzan. She took the jug that was on the bedside table and began to pour.

" I was eighteen and it was soon to be my sister's wedding. My house was full of excitement, and I was helping my sister with her dress." Estelle said as she began to weave her magic of storytelling.

" Estelle, would you like to come and help pick out a spot beside the lake for the wedding?" Estelle's sister Charmaine asked. " Oh, I would love to." Charmaine, Estelle and their mother loaded into the car and began their journey to the lake. It was a beautiful spring day; the weather was clear, and the air was sweets with the scent of Honeysuckle, and the sounds of baby birds could be heard as they carried on the breeze. As the car pulled into the field beside the lake the vision of wild blossoms caught their eyes. " It's beautiful," Estelle whispered trying to not break the sounds of nature.

The three women walked through the flowers and made their way to the lake. They spent hours walking around the lake trying to find the perfect spot, but as the day began to slip away a small grove of trees caught Estelle's eye. " Look, over there," she yelled then running over to them. As Estelle and Charmaine entered the grove they felt as though they had walked into heaven. In the middle of the grove stood a weeping willow with a vine of pale pink and white flowers that hung most delicately. On the surrounding trees grew vines of wild roses and through the grass grew sprays of tiny white flowers that

Shon in the setting sunlight. " It's perfect," Charmaine said as she continued to gaze at the picturesque sight that lay before her. The returned to the car still taken by the sight of the grove.

An hour later the three women returned home to tell the rest of the family what they had seen, and it was settled, the wedding was to be held at the lake. With only two days left there was still a lot to do, like the dress to finish and the food to finish organising for the reception.

" Are you nervous?" Estelle asked her sister as they lay out the gown. " Well, a bit, but also excited." " You're going to look just beautiful," Estelle's mother said as she walked into the room, " Oh dear, I think I'm going to cry." " Mother, don't you dare," Charmaine said. Then at that moment all three women were startled by a car horn outside of Charmaine's window. " Who is it?" Charmaine asked Estelle. Estelle ran to the window and stuck her head out to see. " Oh no, it's Keith." Turning with shock to her mother, " What'll I do, he can't see me yet." " Now don't panic, Estelle go get your father to deal with Keith," instructed their mother. Estelle rushed downstairs slamming the door behind her, shot through the kitchen and the Living room to the front door. " Hi Estelle, is Char..." " What are you doing here," Estelle quickly cutting him off, " You can't see her till the wedding." " Don't worry I'm here to see your father," Keith explained. " Well, you better wait here then," Estelle instructed as she pointed to a chair in the hallway and giving him a suspicious look. Estelle wondered around the corner of the living room, so she could keep an eye on him. " Father!" she hollered, " Father, Keith is here."

Mr Banks came marching up the back path and through the kitchen. " Where is he?" he asked. " I left him by the front door," Estelle said pointing. " Run along and help your mother and Charmaine," he instructed. Estelle rolled her eyes and ran up the staircase to Charmaine's room and knocked on door. " Who is it?" a voice from behind asked. " It's me Estelle." She entered the room shutting the door behind her. " Where's Keith?" Charmaine questioned. " I left him downstairs with father." " Let's get started we've only a few hours before the wedding," their mother said as she hurried the two girls along.

" Charmaine, its time," said her mother as she finished pinning the lace veil. " Mother, dad's waiting in the car," Estelle said as she opened the door to her sister's room and then froze when seeing her sister. " Oh Charmaine, you're beautiful," she said as she found herself overcome with the vision of her sister. " You really think so?" Charmaine asked with a tone of uncertainty in her voice. " Oh yes." " Quickly now, or we'll be late," said their mother as the car horn sounded. All three ladies made their way to the car that was waiting to take them to the lake, where Keith and the rest of the family and friends awaited the bride.

They finally arrived at the lake, with satin ribbons floating and waving in the air. The car pulled up a few yards from the small grove of trees where everyone patiently waited. As Charmaine stepped out of the car it was like watching an angel descend from heaven, her long brown hair spiralled down to her waist with a crown of tiny white blossoms that sat around her head. She wore an ivory lace gown that gently flowed around her body with a soft satin sash that tied in a bow around her hip. As Keith turned to see his bride his heart filled with joy at the sight of the heavenly figure that stood before him, they both gave a gentle smile then turned to face the priest. Time stood still as the vows and promises were made and all the could be heard was the whisper of a breeze through the trees and the gently humming of bees in the distance.

" I now pronounce you husband and wife," announced the priest then placing Charmaine's hand in Keith's. Charmaine and Keith gently kissed and the turned to face their family and friends that gathered for this special occasion. Everyone clapped and cheered and began to toss rice, Estelle ran up and kissed her sister on the cheek and then Keith, Estelle was followed by her father and mother and then Keith's family followed. " Come on girls," Charmaine called as she ran out of the grove. All the single young women gathered outside of the trees ready to catch the bouquet. Estelle took her place at the front of the group and stood at the ready. Charmaine turned, closed her eyes and then tossed the bouquet. It flew into the air, everyone ran towards open ground ready to catch the bouquet as it fell, Estelle picked her skirt and ran with all her might then jumping into the air and catching it as it began to descend. " I've got!" she yelled as took hold of it with both hands. " You know they say the one who catches the bouquet is the next to marry," Charmaine yelled from the other side of the group. " We'll see," Estelle said with a light chuckle. Estelle walked back to the car ready to go home for the reception, as she opened the car door she looked up and saw that John Cavanagh her best friend was watching her, he smiled and dipped his hat, so she smiled back and hollered, " Don't you be getting any ideas either." John's grin widened with a small glimpse of teeth showing, as she climbed into the car she noticed something in John's eyes a look she had never seen before, a look that meant more than friendship. Estelle closed the door and waved to John smelling the bouquet of flowers as the car moved on.

The reception was almost at an end and Estelle began to think back to the ceremony and the look in John's eyes, it sent a warm sensation down her back that made her smile. She walked to the back gate that sat at the end of the garden leaving the party behind she began to study the surrounding trees that lay at the border of her father's property, and in the corner of her eye she noticed John standing beside a large tree that she and he once played in as children. She pushed open the old gate and walked over to him. " Why don't you come over to the party?" she asked. " Well; I'd rather just sit here with you and watch the sunset," he replied as he looked up at the golden rays that lit up the sky. " John." " Yes Estelle." " We've been friends for a long time now," Estelle said being the forward type of girl she is, " I was wondering, if you had started having feelings for me." " What sort of feelings," John said knowing exactly what she meant.

" Well, I started having feelings for you that tell me I want to be more than friends," she explained, " and I was wondering if you maybe felt the same way about me." With his eyes full of love John leaned forward and whispered in her ear, " Estelle, I love you," and the gently kissed her on the cheek. John and Estelle both settled at the bottom of the tree hand in hand and watched the sun slowly sink beneath the horizon.

Chapter 3

Once night had fallen and everyone had left the party John and Estelle walked to the back gate, held each other than kissed and parted ways until the next time they should meet. Estelle wondered back into the house trying to hide the girlish grin that lay upon her face, but the way she felt made it difficult as for the first time she had fallen in love and felt it's heavenly touch.

" Estelle," Charmaine called. Still thinking about what happened she did not hear her sister calling. " Estelle!" Charmaine's voice was louder this time. Jumping at the sound Estelle gathered her thoughts and ran to where her sister was waiting. " So where have you been all this time?" Charmaine question with a suspicious tone. " Oh, nowhere," she answered as she looked out a nearby window. " By the way you could have asked John to come over and join the party." Charmaine said with a smile. " What makes you think I was with John." " I have eyes Estelle, I too wasn't paying much attention to the party, I saw the way he looked at you at the lake," she said placing an arm around her sister's shoulders. Estelle retired to bed that night dreaming of things to come, her heart was filled with love and joy and butterflies of excitement.

She woke the next morning with a smile spread across her face. " Estelle honey, breakfast is almost ready," her mother called from the bottom of the staircase. " I'll be down in a few minutes," Estelle answered as she brushed her hair. " Hello Mrs Cavanagh," she addressed herself as she looked into the mirror already making up her mind to marry John. She then placed the brush on the Tallboy and hurried herself down to the kitchen.

" Good morning father dear," she said as she sat down at the kitchen table. " I know why she's so happy," said her younger brother. " You hush up!" snapped Estelle. " Estelle that's enough," her mother said in an ordering tone. " Well, doesn't anyone want to know why Estelle is so happy?" Jack asked. " Nobody wants to know," Estelle said standing up with fists on the table. " I do Jack," his father said, " Sit down Estelle." " It's about John too," Jack said with a smile looking over to Estelle, " John and Estelle were sitting together under a tree they were holding hands and kissing."

Estelle stood up from the table and ran out of the room to the front veranda where she sat herself on the porch swing trying to keep back any tears the filled her eyes. `She looked down to the track that lead to the main road, feeling the need to run as far as she could but kept her seat as where would she go, then with a glimpse her eye caught the sight of someone walking down the track, at first it was hard to see who it was but as the figure came closer it became clear to see, it was John.

Estelle's face lit up with joy, she jumped out of the swing and shot down the front steps. John began running toward Estelle both holding out their arms to each other, they embrace a short way down the track and then gently kissed. " I missed you," John said with a gentle voice. " Oh, I missed you too," Estelle replied as she looked up into his eyes. " Let's walk a while," John said taking her by the hand. They both walked to the stream that ran through the back of the property where nothing but the sound of running water and birds could be heard.

" It's so beautiful this time of year, I wish it could last forever," Estelle said as she picked the wild daisies that grew alongside the stream. John walked over to Estelle and gave her his hand to help her up from the streams edge, as she rose a light breeze teased the hem of her dress. " John," she said as she leaned her head into his chest. " Yes Estelle," he answered as he stroked her hair. " Promise me you'll never leave me." " I could never leave you Estelle for I will always be with you no matter what may come." John answered as he wrapped his arms around her.

They both followed the stream till the midday sun filled the sky with the warmth of its rays. They stopped to rest in the shade of an old oak tree, with branches that spread across the stream and vines of tiny white blossoms hanging from each branch. " It's true garden of Eden," Estelle said as the spring air filled her lungs. " Remember when we played here as children, we used to get into so much trouble and have so much fun," John said as he looked across the running water. Still holding the flowers in her hand Estelle approached the stream. " Where are you going?" he asked. " Nowhere, just seeing if the stepping stones are still here." Estelle leaned over stream's edge into the water. " They've probably washed away after all these years," John saying as he leaned back against the tree. " I don't believe it, they are still here," she shouted as she began walking across them. " Estelle, you better be careful you might slip," he cautioned her as he stood. " Don't worry I'll be fine," she announced as she reached the middle of the stream. Remembering there was a deep hole in the middle she pretended to lose her balance. " John!" she cried, " Hurry." John jumped to his feet and ran to the edge of the stream and then onto the stepping stones. " I'm coming Estelle," he yelled as he came closer. She was trying so hard not to laugh while at the same time trying to make it look real. As John reached out for Estelle's hand to stop her from falling, with both hands latched onto him she pulled him into the water.

As they sank beneath the water's surface Estelle wasn't sure if he was going to laugh or explode with anger, so she quickly calmed her laughter by dropping her mouth below the water so only her eyes could be seen. His waterlogged body slowly raised out of the water and began to drift towards the bank. Unsure of what he was thinking, Estelle slowly approaches him. " John," she quietly called. John with his back turned smiled and continued to ignore her knowing that she hated it. Trying to play it back Estelle stormed out of the stream and back toward home.

She began counting the seconds before John would come running after her. " Estelle," he yelled, " Estelle come on, I'm sorry." Hearing him call she continued walking knowing he would come after her. She bent to pick some flowers to make a halo, and as she bent John ran up behind her and grabbed her around the waist and causing them to both fall to the ground. " I guess I deserve that," Estelle said as she rolled onto her back to face him. " You bet you did." He said as he lay beside her. " We better dry out before we head back for home," she suggested looking over to John. " Do you think the stream will be here in ten years," she questioned. " Sure, it will be, who would want to destroy something this beautiful." " You're right, it is beautiful, you'd have to be mad to take away something like this," she said sitting up looking around at the surroundings.

As the warm mid-afternoon breeze began to blow their sun-dried clothes Estelle rose to her feet then pulling John to his. " We had better get going, it's getting late," she said looking into his eyes. " Well, we better make a start you never know what may happen to a beautiful young woman such as yourself, so I shall be your escort," John said holding out his arm. The two young lovers reached the start of the dirt driveway that led to Estelle's house, so the two parted with a kiss and went on their way.

" You're just in time dear," Estelle's mother said then smiling, " I'm about to set out supper, go wash your hands." Estelle returned the smile and said, " I love you mama." Then ran out to the back porch to wash. " Jack! come inside I won't call you again."

A few moments later everyone was seated at the table. " Henry, would you please say grace," aske his wife. Estelle, Jack and their mother bowed their heads and closed their eyes and their father began. " Dear lord, we are thankful for the day we have been given, and for the food that has been placed upon our table, we pray that it will be blessed to strengthen our bodies. Oh, and we are also thankful for young John for bringing Estelle home safely, amen. Estelle's father looked up and gave her a wink.

There was total silence at the table, not even Jack would speak as he was still a bit sore from his punishment that morning, then the silence was broken. " Father," Estelle whispered, " I wish to apologize for running out this morning." Estelle stopped and looked over to her mother, her mother nodded, so she continued to eat. " It was unforgivable your temper, but because you had a good reason for it you are forgiven." Her father said then continued to eat. Estelle helped her mother with the dishes and the cleaning of the kitchen so that desert may be prepared. " Here, take this into your father I'll be in soon." Her mother handed her a piece of chocolate cake. " Thank you, mum," Estelle said with a smile, " Thank you for everything."

Chapter 4

" Billy, Jenny, hurry up or we'll be late." Suzan called as she set the table for breakfast. The two children came running down the hall and into the kitchen." Mummy, when are we going to see grandma?" Jenny asked." Just as soon as we've finished breakfast and cleaned up."

" Mrs Cavanagh, Mrs Cavanagh," a voice called to Estelle. Light slowly crept into the darkness of her eyes as she began to open them." Mrs Cavanagh," the voice echoed once again." Your daughter is here to see you." The nurse assisted Estelle to be ready for her daughter." Would you like me to brush your hair?" the nurse asked while straightening the pillows." Thank you dear," Estelle answered with a smile. As the nurse began to brush a knock was heard at the door and then Suzan and the children entered the room." I'll leave you now Mrs Cavanagh," the nurse said then leaving the brush on the bedside table.

" Oh, mum it's so good to see you, and you look so much better than last week." Suzan leaned in to kiss her mother's cheek." Grandma, when are you coming home?" Billy asked." Not for some time yet dear, the doctor thinks I'm not well enough just yet," she explained." Here's some money you two go down to the canteen and see what you can find," Suzan handed the two children equal amounts of money and sent them on their way." Suzan," Estelle reached out to her daughter's hand." "Yes mum."

"When I'm well enough to leave the hospital, I intend to go back to Summerfield, only for a few days or at least for when the snow falls." Estelle remembering how beautiful it was." Are you sure you want to do this mum, it's such a long way to travel and you might end up in hospital again," Suzan said as she sat upon the bed holding her mother's hand." Please Suzan, it's all I want to do before my time is to come," she explained.

" Tell you what, I'll talk to the doctor and see what he recommends." " Thank you so much, you make me so happy," Estelle spoke with a soft calm voice. " I'll be back in a few minutes, I had better go and get the kids and see what Doctor Hardings has to say," Suzan said then kissing her mother's forehead.

As Estelle lay there awaiting her verdict, she began to think of her beautiful field of flowers and how she longed to see them, to smell and to touch them once again. A small tear rolled down her cheek as the image of her loved one passed filled her head. " Oh John, how I miss you so," she gently whispered.

Suzan eventually found the doctor, she hesitated for a moment and then said. " Doctor, I know it's probably impossible, but mum was wondering, well she was actually hoping she could visit Summerfield." Summerfield, why?" he questioned. " She wants to see the places she once lived as a girl.... " " Are we going away mummy," Jenny interrupted. " No Jenny." " Well, I can't really guarantee anything yet, but we'll see how she gets along."

Suzan and the children made their way back to Estelle's room, Billy and Jenny ran ahead to get their first. " Billy,

Jenny, stop running you know there's sick people in here," Suzan quietly raising her voice. The two came running into the room yelling, " Grandma, grandma we're going on a holiday." " Hold it right there you two, I don't know if we are just yet," Suzan said cutting them off before they could say any more. " Mum I've spoken to the doctor, and he said it will be a few more weeks before you can leave the hospital and even then, you have to take it easy," Suzan trying to make out everything would be ok. " I don't know what I would do without you," Estelle said as she smiled. " We better go now mum we've been long enough, and you need to rest if we are going to travel." Suzan leaned in and kissed her mother's cheek as did the children. " We'll try come in tomorrow, love you mum." Estelle drifted off to sleep with a small feeling of excitement of things to come.

" Happy Birthday!" everyone shouted. Estelle's face lit up with surprise, she had thought everyone had forgotten her birthday. " Oh, mum this is wonderful thank you so much," she said as she gave her mother a big hug. " Is Charmaine coming?" " I really don't know, I sent her a letter, but I never heard back," her mother paused for a moment then continued, " well never mind that now if she turns up, she turns up. Come on let's get back to the party."

Half an hour had passed and still no sign of her sister, their mother was starting to worry as Charmaine was close to giving birth. Then through the backdoor a familiar voice was heard. " Well, where's the birthday girl." Dropping everything she help Estelle ran out to the back door. " Charmaine!" Estelle shouted, " you came." Then throwing her arms around her sister. " I wouldn't dream of missing your birthday for anything," she said as they both walked back into the living room. " Oh, mum this is the best birthday I think I've ever had, just to have all of you here is plenty enough." Estelle said trying her best to hold back tears of joy. " Did John come around?" Charmaine questioned. " Ah no, he was unable to come, his family moved away," explained their mother. " Oh, where to?" " Melbourne." " Oh Estelle, I'm so sorry, " Charmaine said reaching out for her sister's hand. " May I be excused, I'm going up to my room," Estelle said as she wiped a tear from her cheek.

Estelle lay upon her bed reading a letter she had received a few days earlier; her heart was aching at the loneliness she felt from John's absence. The feelings of spring love filled her mind of what she and John had shared the season before. " Estelle honey," her mother called " could you please come down here, I need some help to clean up."

Not answering she carefully folded the letter and placed it in her dresser draw then making her way down to the living room. She collected a few dishes that lay around the room. As she was leaving the room she sang out over her shoulder, " Hi John." In that instance sounds of dishes came crashing to the floor, Estelle's head popped out from around the corner of the kitchen door, her eyes lit up with so much excitement they looked like they were about to pop. " JOHN!" She screamed then throwing herself into his arms. A small crystal-like tear fell from her eye and slipped to the corner or her mouth. " You didn't think I'd miss your twenty second birthday did you," John said as he stroked her hair. " Well, you live so far away I didn't think you would be able to make it." " When it comes to you, my Estelle, no distance is too far." " Come on you two let's get a photograph, Estelle you move to the right and John place both arms around her so both Estelle's hands are inside yours," her mother instructed, " now smile." Jack came running into the room trying to be as gentlemanly as possible for a twelve-year-old can be saying " Well, when are you two to be married?". " Wait till I get my hands-on you Jack Banks," Estelle hollered. Jack then ran flat tack out of the room laughing.

" Estelle," John said as he turned her to face him. " Yes John." John then knelt before her gently taking her hands into his. " John, what are you doing?" Estelle questioned with a strange look on her face. " Estelle, we have been the best of friends our entire life, and I could not have been happier to have a friend such as you, we have had so many adventures together and I have now reached the time where I want to start a new adventure with not only my best friend, my one true soul mate, my one true love. So, with all to witness I come to you on bended knee, Estelle Banks would you do me the greatest honour of giving me your hand in marriage and becoming my wife?" John spoke in a soothing voice.

Estelle stood there motionless, eyes wide open and mouth gaping. " Please say yes, my knee is killing me," John pleaded. Estelle let out a big scream and yelled as loud as she could, " YES! yes John Cavanagh, I will marry you." John jumped to his feet then picking up Estelle as he hugged her, both laughing like fools as he spun her around. " What is it?" Estelle's mother said as she ran into the room. " Mum. John and I are..." Estelle paused. " Yes, what is it?" questioned her mother. " John and I are getting married," Estelle announced trying to hold back her excitement. Instantly her mother let out a scream and threw her arms around John and then

Estelle. Charmaine slowly entered the room with both hands resting on the hollow of her back. " Hey, what's all the excitement?" " Oh, Charmaine isn't it wonderful." Her mother said turning to her. " Isn't what wonderful." Charmaine said as she struggled to sit in the chair. " I'm so sorry, I'm just so happy John just proposed to your sister and she said yes," explained her mother. " Well, it's about time." " What do you mean it's about time," Estelle said? " I've seen this coming for some time now, especially the night of my wedding, I saw you two sitting under the tree out back." Charmaine said as she raised an eyebrow. " Ahh mum." Charmaine's breathing grew deeper. " What is it dear." " My water just broke, I think it's time," she said placing both hands around her belly. " Estelle run out to the barn and get your father, John, could you go find Jack for me, and I'll go collect some things for the hospital," instructed their mother who was always good in an emergency or any other crisis.

Everybody loaded into two cars and made their way to the hospital breaking every speed limit. " Are we nearly there yet," Charmaine screamed for the back seat. Reaching the hospital everyone poured out of the cars and spilled into the hospital. " Jack," said their mother, " you come with me." " Where are we going?" " To find a doctor." Jack and his mother ran down the corridor look for the doctor but instead finding a nurse. " Oh, Sister excuse me," called Mrs Banks in a calm voice. The nurse not hearing kept on walking. " NURSE! " Mrs Banks yelled with the deepest roughest voice. The nurse stopped dead in her tracks and turned to face Mrs Banks and Jack. " How can I help you," the spoke in a superior tone. " My daughter is about to give birth in your waiting room, could you please locate me a doctor." " It won't be easy as all the doctors are out on call," the nurse explained, " I'm sorry but you'll just have to wait until one is available." Jack grabbed the nurse's watch that was pinned to her uniform and pulled her down to his level. " Listen lady, if you don't get a doctor here in five seconds, I'm gonna make you wish you weren't a nurse," Jack said as he looked her in the eye and started to show his teeth with a rather wide grin. " Jack!" his mother's voice filled with a surprised tone. " Well, that goes double for me," Jack's mother said. " I'll see if I can page one," replied the nurse as she straightened herself and her uniform. " Mrs banks, we found a doctor," John yelled as he approached. " You're a lucky lady," Jack said to the nurse looking up through his eyebrows. Jack, his mother and John ran back to the waiting room to be with Mrs Banks while Charmaine was in the delivery room.

What seemed like hours was only minutes. Everyone was pacing anxiously to know what was happening. After half an hour a nurse came out holding a baby girl. " Mrs Banks," the nurse called as she stepped forward. Charmaine's mother took the baby in her arms and held it like it was her own, then a few moments later another nurse came out holding another baby this time a boy. " Oh Mrs Banks," the nurse said as she walked into the room, " Your daughter Charmaine has had twins." Then in unison like a choir the entire family said " TWINS!" and then there was a loud thump on the floor, everyone turned to see and when they did there lay Mr Banks flat on his back and out like a light, everybody burst into laughter.

Two orderlies helped Mr Banks to a nearby chair. " Estelle fan your father " instructed her mother. Estelle sat next to her father fanning rapidly trying to bring him round. Mr Banks eyes began to creep open. " What happened?" Mr Banks asked as he looked around the room. " You fainted daddy," Estelle said as she kept on fanning. " That's impossible, I'm a man and men don't faint," Mr Banks said as he strengthened his voice. " Well now that you've decided to join us from not fainting, would you like to hold one of your grandchildren." Mrs Banks said walking up with a baby in each arm.

The small family huddled around the two babies, adoring and pinching their little bodies. " Mrs Banks you may see your daughter now," the doctor announced. " Who?" Mrs Banks replied. " Your daughter, Charmaine." " Oh, yes, of course," Mrs Banks forgetting for a moment having a daughter. " Hi mum," Charmaine said as her mother entered the room. "How are you feeling dear?" Her mother pulled a chair closer to the bed and took Charmaine's hand. " Just a little tired, but quite happy." " Well, you get rested and I'll come see you tomorrow." Her mother rose from the chair and kissed Charmaine on the cheek, her face lit up with so much joy and happiness she began to cry. The nurse handed Charmaine's daughter to her and the sat upon the bed holding her son. " They are beautiful children Mrs Maddison," the nurse commented. " They are indeed." Charmaine said gazing at both babies. " I'll leave you to it as I better get back to work," the nurse said placing the baby she held into a crib next to the bed. By the end of the week Charmaine had gained her strength and returned home with two healthy babies.

Six months had passed, and plans were under way for Estelle's wedding. Excitement had filled the hair as the wedding was set for spring. " Mum, were you nervous?"

Estelle questioned. " Well, not at first but as time grew closer yes very much so. It's quite natural to feel this way dear you'll even start to doubt your decision.

John and Estelle came across a small white chapel with a bell tower out front. " You know with a little work on the gardens and a bit of paint, this place could be perfect for the wedding," John said walking closer to the little building. " John it's perfect. we could even place more stepping stones in the path. It's going to look beautiful." The next few months the entire family worked on the little chapel, painting, planting and repairing, ready for mid spring. Three weeks before the wedding the chapel was complete and was certainly a sight to be seen. Roses growing strong on either side of the entrance, small hedges were taking shape alongside the footpath, the white exterior of the little building shone in the sunlight and the bell sparkled as it reflected the light. So, the family celebrate with a big picnic on the chapel grounds.

A hush fell upon the valley of Summerfield, all that could be herd was the sound of wild finches and the light rustling of the trees as they danced in the spring breeze. The music played, Estelle and her father entered the little chapel, a pin drop could be heard from the silence of the guests. John slowly turned to see his beloved glide down the flower lined aisle toward him, it was though a spell had been cast upon the chapel. Estelle's gown flowed upon the light breeze that came through the tiny chapel and the scent of wild jasmine teased the senses of everyone it touched John grew breathless at the beauty of Estelle.

Mr Banks and Estelle reached the altar and placed his daughter's hands into John's hands and gave Estelle a kiss on her forehead. The two young lovers then took the last few steps and approached the priest and the ceremony began. Both Mrs. Banks and Mrs. Maddison began to cry even Charmaine shed a tear. The love from Estelle and John could be felt in everyone.

Chapter 5

" Mum." Estelle could hear her daughter's voice echoing in her head. She slowly opened her eyes to see her daughter Suzan sitting on the bed beside her. " Hello dear, you're early today," Estelle said thinking of visiting hours and the crappy nurse that works the morning shift. " Mum, did you forget you're leaving today." " Where am I going?" she questioned with a puzzled voice. " Home mum, to Summerfield Valley." A smile crept across Estelle's face, " Are we really going?" "Yes mum. Doctor Hardings said it would be ok and I thought we could go now so you could see your field of flowers before it was time for the first snowfall. " Thank you, Suzan, thank you so much," Estelle said as she began to tear.

Suzan and an orderly escorted Estelle to the car and awaiting children. " Grandma isn't it exciting," Jenny hollered as she hung out of the car window. Billy quickly opened the car door to allow his grandmother to sit in the front. With the help of the orderly Estelle carefully climbed into the car at the same time saying, " Hell, life's a bitch when you're old and sick." The two children giggled at the sound of a curse word. " Mum! please not in front of the kids. " Oh, it's not you've never said a bad word." Estelle said glancing up from her seat belt. Suzan pulled out of the hospital parking bay and started their search for Summerfield Valley.

" How long do you think it will take to get there?" Estelle asked as she wiped some sweat from her forehead.
" Well. We've only been on the road for a few hours

mum, so we are looking at least another ten to twelve hours drive, so maybe everyone should get some sleep for now." Suzan explained. " Mum I'm hungry," Jenny said leaning forward over the front seat. " We'll get something as soon as we reach the next service station." Estelle fell into a deep sleep and drifted off to her memories.

" Happy Anniversary!" John said as he leaned over to kiss Estelle good morning. " Hi there, Mr Cavanagh." She said as she gazed into John's eyes. " Do you realise Mrs Cavanagh that we have now been married for three years." John said stroking her hair. " Wait there." John got off the bed and walked over to his coat that hung on the coat rack and returned with his hand closed. " Now close your eyes and don't open them till I say. One, two, three, now open." A silver locket sat in his hand glistening in the morning sun as it came through the bedroom window. " Oh John, it's beautiful." Estelle opened the locket and inside there was a picture of John and an inscription that read... " To my dearest love forever in my heart you'll be, John." " I too have something for you, something I know you'll love. So, are you ready for it?" she said taking a deep breath. " John, I'm pregnant, we are going to have a baby."

There was a short silence in the room and then John let out a yell. " Woohoo! wait, are you sure? how long? when did you find out? John asked as he sat back onto the bed. " Two months, I didn't want to tell you before I wanted to keep it a surprise for now and let me tell you it wasn't easy." " Well, my lovely, it was a surprise worth waiting for." John said with the biggest grin then hugging her.

" Ok John you can stop hugging me now, I'm beginning to lose circulation in my legs." " Oh sorry. Are you ok? How do you feel?" " John I'm fine, really, I can still do everything like I did before." She said laying her hand upon the side of his face. John never looked so happy before, besides the day they married, and the radiance from the good news just shone from the young couple. As the months slowly drifted by John and Estelle were counting the months, the weeks and the days that were left till the birth of their first child.

Spring had finally arrived, and it wasn't long till it was time. Estelle was prepared for her time in hospital. " John, do you have to go? there's only a week till the baby comes." " Angel I'm sorry, I did everything I could to get out of it, but the boss wouldn't hear about it, I'm pretty sure I'll be back in time to be with you. I'll call you as soon as I arrive. Ok?" " Well, ok but as soon as you arrive and not a minute after. I need to know everything went ok." She said as she took hold of her husband's hand. Standing on the front porch they gazed deeply into each other's eyes as though it was the last time they would see one another. John leaned into Estelle and kissed her gently then placing his arms around her. " I love you Estelle, more than anything in this world, and I promise I will be back in time to be with you." He kissed her once again and climbed into the waiting taxi. The two waved to each other as the car drove out of sight, a tear rolled down Estelle's cheek and the only sound she could hear was the sound of her heartbeat grow louder. For the first time she felt alone.

Two days had passed and there had been no word from John and slight panic had begun to fill Estelle's head. A third day went by and still no word. She knew something was wrong, she could feel it deep within her soul. With a loud ringing of the doorbell Estelle woke with a fright, once again the doorbell rang. She slowly lifted her weary body from the armchair and made her way to the door, recalling her loved one's absence she took a deep breath and opened it. " Mamma, it's you, please come in." " Oh, honey are you ok?" asked her mother. "Yeah, I'm holding out, only a few more days to go." " Where's John honey, is he at the market? " " No, he's overseas on a business trip in New York, he said he'll be back in time for the birth but I'm starting to get a bit worried, I haven't heard from him in three days and just have the sickest feeling that something has gone wrong." " Estelle, maybe he's just forgotten to call, or he just hasn't had a moment to spare to get to a phone yet," her mother trying to comfort her. " Come, I'll make us some tea, you really need to try not stress at this stage." " Mum, he said he would call as soon as he arrived, he promised."

Estelle and her mother were interrupted by a loud knock on the door. " Just a minute," Estelle called. Estelle and her mother approached the front door. " Good afternoon, ma'am, are you Mrs John Cavanagh?" " I am Mrs Cavanaugh." Estelle said opening the door wider. " I am Detective Harris, and this is my partner Detective Kelly." Announced the police detective as he displayed his badge. Estelle's face filled with fear and tears began to stream down her face, she let out a scream as she fell to her knees, and she could feel her heart die for she knew the reason why the two detectives had come to see her.

" Ma'am," Detective Harris said as he knelt to help her. Detective Kelly stepped forward to speak to Mrs Banks. "

Ma'am, the plane Mr Cavanagh was on to New York went down three hundred miles before it reached the States, no survivors have been found. Please accept our condolences." " Mrs Cavanagh, if there's anything we can do for you or help you with please let us know and we will do what we can." " I'm sure we can manage. Thank you, thank you both." Estelle's mother said as she showed the detectives the door.

" MOTHER!" Estelle screamed. A pool of blood could be seen where Estelle lay, she screamed again, her mother turned. " Oh god, not this, not now. Detectives wait! it's my daughter, I think she's gone into early labour." Her mother and both Detectives gently placed Estelle into the back of the police car. " Please hurry, she's lost a lot of blood." Estelle's mother said as she held her close. Some moments later they arrived at the hospital, Detective Kelly ran into emergency to get assistance. " Hurry there's an emergency. A woman had come into early labour and looks like she's lots a lot of blood." Hollered Detective Kelly as he reached the front desk. Estelle's screams could be heard through the E.R. doors, tears flooded down her face. Her mother and Detective tried their best to comfort her. " Estelle baby it won't be much longer, help is coming." Her mother said as she held her close to her chest.

Detective Harris lifted her from the car and began to carry Estelle into the hospital, A Doctor and several nurses met the Detective, Mrs Banks and Estelle at the glass doors that divided the outside world to that of the sanctuary of the hospital. With speed and agility Estelle's weak body was carefully placed upon the awaiting bed. " Nurse Thomas, prepare the I.C.U. and the O.R. " the doctor turned and said, " Ma'am, Sir, you'll have to wait here." " How long before we know anything?" Estelle's mother trembled. " I'm not too sure as yet, we have to see what damage has been done, we'll let you know as soon as soon as we know something, so please take a seat it's now a waiting game, we will do everything we can for your daughter." The doctor turned and ran to the Operating Room.

" Ma'am, come sit down I'm sure the staff here are doing all they can for her." Detective Harris and Kelly waited with Mrs Banks to try bringing her comfort. Estelle's pain could be heard in the waiting room; Mrs Banks lost her breath at the fear for her daughter's moment of trial. " Detective Harris, what could be taking them so long. They've been in there for two hours, what if something's wrong?" " Ma'am, please stay calm and think positive, I'm sure both your daughter and her baby will be fine, this is the finest hospital in the county. Would you like some coffee or maybe some tea?" Det. Harris offered. " Ah, yes, please. Tea would be nice." " I'll get it," Det. Kelly said, " I'll get us all one." " Detective Harris." " Ma'am, please call me Marc." " Very well. Marc, I am very thankful for all the help you have given me and my daughter..." " Pardon me ma'am." The doctor said as he entered the room. " Your daughter is doing fine, and you have a very beautiful granddaughter. They are both in recovery." " Can I see her now?" Mrs Banks asked sighing with some relief. " Certainly, if you'd like to come with me I'll take you to her." " I'll wait here." Det. Harris said as he took a seat. " Oh, please come, I'm sure she'll be most happy to see you." Estelle's mother and Detective Harris entered the quiet hospital room where the exhausted young woman lay resting. " Estelle honey, it's me, your mother." Her mother stroked her hair as she looked down upon her tired face. " Mamma. Where

am I? " You're in hospital. You just had your baby."
" I did? What did I have?" Estelle softly spoke. " You had
a very beautiful and healthy girl." A small tear made its
way down Estelle's cheek and moistened her pillow.

Still in a daze from the past events, Estelle glanced
around the semi dark room, the detective Marc Harris
was standing in the shadows at the end of her bed, his
face could not be seen. " Oh John, I knew you'd make it,
I just knew... " " Ah, honey, this is Detective Harris. You
remember him, don't you?" said Mrs Banks as she
stepped forward and taking her daughter's hand. " Oh
yes; I remember now." Estelle recalling everything as
she looked away. " Maybe I should give you both some
time alone," Detective Harris said as he walked to the
door.
" No, please stay, after all if it wasn't for you and your
partner I probably wouldn't be here."

Time past on for Estelle and her daughter, and the
horrifying news of John's death was now just a memory,
but the memory of her first love and beloved husband
was still very strong and filled her heart every day. There
were times where Estelle would just sit and lose herself
in her memories of the day of John's proposal and when
they would sit under the large tree out back and talk of
things to come and how their future would be as Mr. and
Mrs. Cavanagh.

Sixteen years had passed; Estelle, her mother and the
rest of her family were preparing for Suzan's sixteenth
birthday celebration. Grandmother Banks was in the
kitchen cooking up a storm, Estelle's brother Jack was
clearing the back garden to set out the table, Father
Banks was getting the wood together for the open fire pit

and Estelle and Suzan were hanging streamers and paper lanterns from tree to tree across the garden. Once the working bee had stopped they all stood back and took it all in.

" It's wonderful. Thank you so much." Suzan hugged her mother with such gratitude Estelle's eyes began to tear up. " Anything for you my angel," and she kissed her daughter on the forehead. " I'm sure father would have thought so to. Do you think he is here today?" Suzan asking holding her mother's hands. " Angel, he wouldn't miss it for the world."
" I understand today must be hard for you mum, being it was to this day dad, well." Suzan paused before saying more. " Suzan, yes, it is, but it's ok, I'm ok. You see, I have you a wonderful image of your father every time I look at you. He's in your smile, your eyes and sometimes in your laughter, but most of all in our hearts where he will always live on."

In the distance cars could be heard as they drove down the track that led to the house, and so the family quickly finished doing their few chores in time for the guests. Estelle stood inside the living room watching through the window as Suzan ran out to the front gate to start greeting her friends, her mind wondered a little and a smile came to her eyes. " She's beautiful, you have done well." A voice gently spoke to her ear, and a warm breath could be felt. " Yes, she is. We had made a beautiful young woman, and she is just like you my love, in so many ways. Oh, John, I miss you so much." Estelle said as she placed her hand over her heart. " I am always here my love, you will never be alone for with every beat you feel within I will sweeten with my touch, and if you want to see me just close your eyes and I will be here." A light warm breeze brushed her cheek, and she could smell John's scent and, in that instance, he was gone. Estelle smiled a little more as she touches her cheek and a small tear settled on the tip of her finger. " I love you." She whispered.

" Mother; are you ok?" Suzan asked as she took her mother's hand. " Yes, of course. I'm just marvelling at how lovely you have grown." Suzan embraced her mother, and at the same time Estelle could feel John with them. " Ok, now let's get out back and get things going." Estelle and Suzan wiped away any tears, and both headed to the back garden to the festivities. Streamers and party whistles were being set off. The table was set with sandwiches, slices, cupcakes, and a large punch bowl in the middle. Mr. Banks had started the fire pit and collected long sticks, so the guests could roast marshmallows over the fire, while Mrs. Banks brought out the roast meats and vegetables. The radio played in the background for entertainment and the lanterns were lit, the site was splendid, and laughter could be heard all around. Estelle watched the festivities from the back veranda with a smile and the comfort of the feeling from John by her side. Then she noticed a young man making eyes at Suzan.

 " I remember that look, it was the one I gave to you at your sister's wedding." A whisper touched her ear. Estelle had a giggle. " Oh, I remember, and it was that moment I knew." She stood watching her daughter and this young man as they talked, and just like herself and John they wandered off to sit under that same tree where she and John dreamed of their future.

Time drifted on for Estelle and her family. The seasons changing and children growing up and Estelle could feel the touch of time as the years went by, but the one thing that never changed was her memories. The memories of her time as a girl and of the time most precious to her with her beloved John. She often sat listening to his whispers on the wind and the gentle touch of his hand to her cheek. In the distance of her mind, she could hear the echo of a telephone bell ringing. She came back from her time in the past and looked around the room and then realised where she was, she slowly stood and walked over to the phone.

" Hello?" Estelle spoke into the handset. " Hello Mrs. Cavanagh, this is Toby I'm calling to let you know that Suzan has gone into labour." It was her daughter's husband Toby, " I'm just settling Suzan in, and I will be right out to pick you up, say twenty minutes." Estelle's eyes widened " Oh thank you Toby dear, I'll be ready in the shake of a lamb's whats-it." She could feel her energy pick with the exciting news and went straight to a picture of John. " How exciting my love, there are going to be new children around us, oh you would be so proud of our little girl. Well, no time to waste must get ready." Estelle and Toby arrived at the hospital in record time, Estelle a little befuddled from the drive but in one piece. The two hurried into the birthing ward where Suzan was not too far off giving birth.

"Mum."

        " I'm right here dear, you are doing so well, and I am very proud of you, and you can bet your father is too." Estelle took her daughter's hand and moved some hair from her face.

"Where's Toby?"
" I'm right here angel." he said as he walked to the other side of the bed. " Is there anything you need?" he asked "Are you serious right now!" Suzan let out a scream as another contraction was hitting. Toby stepped back in fear and looked over at Estelle. She gave him a wink and said, " Don't worry dear women are usually like a possessing demon in these situations, it's nothing against you." Are you serious, nothing against him! he did this to me. It's all his fault, and if I wasn't lying here right now, he'd be a few body parts lighter." Suzan screamed again, as the contractions were very close together now. Toby's eyes widened as Suzan glared at him as she screamed once again." "Toby dear, maybe you could go to the canteen and get me a tea please." Estelle asked as she could see he was about to lose it. " Tea, yes tea would be good." He said taking steps towards to door. " Good calming tea."

" Doctor, do you think it will be much longer?" Estelle questioned.
" Well contractions are five minutes apart so hopefully any moment now." He explained. " Ok, I see the head. Now Suzan I'm going to need you to start pushing."
With her face turning red and sweat pouring from her brow she screamed again as she pushed with everything she had. Estelle held her hand tight with one hand and whipped the sweat away with the other and at that moment Toby walked into the room.
" No way." Toby then dropped the teas and hit the floor like a bag of bricks. As Suzan pushed and screamed, she saw Toby on the floor, her eyes widened and at the same time yelled, " Are you friggin kidding me!" and then it happened a little girl was born.

Both Suzan and Estelle cried at the sight of the newborn and Toby finally came around. " We have a little girl, Toby." Suzan spluttered out through the tears." Toby stood and stumbled over to the bed and kissed his wife on the head. " She's beautiful, but um why do you still look pregnant?" he asked. Suzan looked up at him through her brown and said, " Honey you carry one of these around for nine months and see if you fall back into shape." Ten minutes had passed, and Suzan felt the sensation of pressure on her pelvis and then let out a scream.

The Doctor came back into the room. " I was wondering when this was going to happen."   " Happen? What do you mean, happen?" All three of them asked. " What; you didn't know. You're having twins." The doctor explained as he readied himself for the next delivery. " WHAT! ah no, I was told there was only one! Suzan said as she began to breath heavy.
" Ok Suzan you need to start pushing as this one is on its way." Toby took the first baby and sat in a chair off to the side and Estelle once again took her daughter's hand and started to comfort her as best she could. Then in no time she gave birth to the second baby and this time a boy.
" Well congratulations you now have a baby boy." The attending nurse wrapped up the baby and handed him to Suzan.

Tears of joy and exhaustion rolled down her face, the room was full of so much love even the nurse shed a tear.
" Well done my baby." Estelle said as she kissed Suzan in the head. The baby boy let out a cry that sounded like a squeaky toy and was followed by the other baby doing

the same.
" Oh, Suzan I am so proud of you. As if I couldn't be any
happier than I already am." With the other baby in arms
Toby walked over to the bedside and sat in the chair next
to Suzan so both babies could be together. A silence
filled the room and all that could be heard was the soft
sounds of the babies as they breathed.

Chapter 6

" Mum, Mum, it's time to wake up. I'm pulling into a roadside cafe for a bite to eat." Suzan said as lightly tapping her mother's hand. " Have we arrived." Estelle asked as she looked around in a sleepy daze. " Nearly there mum, just over an hour to go. Billy, Jenny, come on guys let's get something to eat." Suzan reaching over to wake the children. The small weary family stumbled into the cafe and stared at the menu that was posted above the counter. With minds boggling at what they read, they finally came to a decision. " Billy, Jenny, what would you like?" Suzan still reading the menu. " Can I have a burger and some fries?" Billy asked. " Me too mummy." " Mum, what would you like to have?" " Oh, I'll just have some carrot cake and coffee." " Hi, my name is Tracey how can I help you?" Announced a young girl from behind the counter. " Yeah, ah, can I get two small burgers with fries, two carrot cakes and two flat whites please." Suzan ordered as she rummaged through her bag. " Will that be everything?" " Oh, and two small milkshakes, one chocolate and one strawberry please." " If you would like to find a table, I'll bring everything out when it's ready." Tracey said as she handed a table number to Jenny.

The little family sat quietly at the table, the two children sipping on their milkshakes and Estelle and Suzan drinking their coffees while waiting for their food as it was placed on the table. " I am so hungry." Billy said as he looked at his burger. " Well, if you're hungry hurry up and eat and you won't be hungry anymore." Suzan said as she organised their plates. " Mum, are you ok?"
" I'm fine dear. Just a little excited I'm finally going home; a place I never thought I'd see again."

Everyone quietly ate their meals with anticipation to complete the long tiresome journey. " Ok, who needs to go to the toilet before we start off again." Suzan asking the children while cleaning up their mess. " Mum, do you need to go?" After refreshing themselves they all piled into the car and began the final stretch of the journey.

" What's that smell mummy?" Jenny asked as she stuck her head out of the window. " It's the wild blossoms that grow in the fields." Estelle explained as she soaked in the freshness. " Will we get to see the flowers mum?" " All in good time Billy, all in good time." " It still looks the same. Just like I remember it." Estelle said as she looked over the scenery they passed. She could see visions of herself and John as they ran through the fields and the fun they had catching frogs in the creek.

" Mum, are you OK?" Suzan noticed a tear glisten in the sunlight as it settled on her mother's-tired cheek. " Oh, I'm fine. I couldn't be happier." Estelle smiled as she continued to watch the endless fields pass by. As the day went on and night began to creep its way in Suzan pulled into a small motel as you entered Summerfield Valley. " Ok. everybody, it's not much I know but it's the only

one they had left." Suzan prepared the tired travellers as she opened the door. " Well, everyone we had better get some sleep, we have a big day tomorrow."
" Goodnight mummy." The two children kissed their mother and jumped into their beds. " We love you."

With the freshness of the air and the singing of the birds, and the soothing warmth of the sun's rays, Estelle's eyes crept open to view the wondrous countryside that was once a memory for what seemed like an eternity. " Billy, Jenny, it's time to wake up," Suzan hollered as she walked into her mother's room, " Mum' it's time to wake up. Oh my god, mum! mother!" Suzan yelled as she ran to the front door. " What's wrong mum?" Billy asked as he rubbed his eyes. " Nothing honey I'll be back in a few minutes." Suzan ran into reception, " Excuse me, please, have you seen my mother this morning, she seems to have wandered off." " Well, I did see and elderly lady going down the street earlier on." " Thank you so much." Suzan then ran off in the same direction to find Estelle.

" Suzan where are you rushing off to?" Estelle questioned her panic-stricken daughter. " Mum, where the hell have you been?" Suzan yelled out. " I'm sorry dear, I was just so excited to be home I went for a little walk down to the store, and don't curse at me. Now, come inside and have some breakfast." " Mum, next time you go somewhere, please let me know, you really had me worried."

Estelle and her family began their search for the places where she once roamed and played as a young girl. The air was crisp and clear, and the chill of winter was beginning to fill the air, but that was not enough to stop Estelle from looking and searching for the memories she desperately held onto, especially the field of wild multicoloured flowers where she and John once spent their youth. " Suzan, may we go back to the motel now, I'm feeling a little tired." Estelle said try to keep her weary eyes from closing. " Yeah sure, are you ok mum?" " Yes, I'm fine, it's probably all the excitement. At my age it's a lot to handle."

The next morning the sun crept its way through an opening in the curtains that hung in Estelle's room, she could hear the sweet song of the morning birds as they echoed in her mind. A smile touched her lips as she heard her John's voice. " Good morning my angel." His voice still sounded like it did the day they married, and she could still smell the cologne he wore and remembered how it made her dizzy. A light gentle breeze touched her cheek, and she knew John was there with her.

" Morning mum. I thought we would go for a picnic at the park today, do you think you would feel up to it?" Suzan asked as she knocked on the bedroom door. " Oh yes, I'm feeling much better thank you and that's a lovely idea." " Mum, I have a small surprise planned for you, I'm sure you will enjoy." Suzan said as she helped her mother into the car.

The two children were busy playing in the playground and Suzan and Estelle gathered the leftover food. " So, where's this surprise I'm supposed to get?" Estelle questioned. " Hello Estelle." A voice came from behind some trees. " Charmaine? Is it really you?" Estelle tearing up as she turned. The two sisters stood for a moment looking at each other, then embraced, both with tears streaming down their faces they held the other

tight not wanting to ever let go. " Hello Estelle."   "
Keith! it's so good to see you again. Thank you, Suzan
this has indeed been the most wonderful day, thank you,
thank you." Estelle then turned and held her daughter.

" Have you been to the field yet?" Charmaine asked as
everyone sat back at the picnic table. " No, not yet. I'm
going to try and get mum there tomorrow." Suzan
explained. " It feels so good to be back in Summerfield."
Charmaine said as she looked around the landscape.
" We better get back to the motel, the air is changing and
it's getting on." Suzan advised. " Suzan, can I speak with
you for a moment," Charmaine took Suzan aside, " How
long does your mother have?"
" Well, it's a little hard to tell, mum's hanging on a fine
thread, she could pass at any given time, the doctor
didn't think she would even get this far."
" Is it that bad?" Charmaine asked as she held back
tears. "Mum wants to go see the flowers tomorrow. Will
you and Keith come with us? I'm sure mum would love
you both to be there."
" We would love to. Well, we had better get going it's
starting to get a little chilly." Charmaine said as she
pulled her shawl around her shoulders.

" Here we are mum. Okay guys both of you carry the
picnic gear in and I'll help grandma." Suzan instructed.
Suzan unbuckled and turned to Estelle. " Mum, we're
back at the motel." She lightly tapped her mother's
hand. " Mum, we're back, oh god no. MUM! wake up
dammit!" Suzan began to scream. " Billy, Jenny, hurry
get in the car we've got to go to the hospital." With
smoke billowing from the tyres Suzan raced to the
hospital as fast as she could without stopping for
anything. She pulled up outside of emergency and ran

inside.   " Please I need help." She yelled but there was no response. " Will someone bloody well help me my mother is dying; she's in the car!" Suzan viciously screamed.

Some moments later Charmaine and Keith arrived at the hospital.
" How is she?" Keith asked.   " I don't know, they haven't told me anything yet. Aunt Charmaine why are they taking so long.”   " Suzan honey, I'm sure they are doing the best they can.”
" Look, here comes a doctor now." Keith said raising to his feet. " Suzan, I'm very sorry but it's not good. The cancer cells have now spread to your mother's brain, and unfortunately there isn't much more that we can do except to give her pain killers to make her as comfortable as possible.”
" So, how much time do you think she has left?" Suzan asked with the swelling of tears in her eyes.”
" Well, twenty-four hours at the most, maybe two days. Well I must go on rounds now but please do not hesitate to page me if there are any problem.”
" Thank you, doctor, can we see her?”
" Sure, but try not to be too long, she really needs to rest.”
" Where are the children?" Keith asked looking around the waiting room.
" They're up in the nursery; I didn't want them to see mum this way."

Suzan entered her mother's room first followed by Charmaine and then by Keith. Suzan sat in the chair that was placed by the bed." Oh mum, you can't go yet. you're so close to where you want to be." She touched

her mother's hand followed by a cry of pain and then a flow of tears. Charmaine could not hold her tears any longer. She held Suzan tight, even that was not enough to ease the pain they both felt.
"Suzan."
" Mum?" Suzan said turning to the pale body that lay before her.
" Suzan, listen to me. I know I don't have much time left, but promise me one thing, please. Before I die take me to the field."
" But mum it's said to snow any day now."
" Please, promise me. it's the only thing I want before it's too late." Estelle begged with what breath she could manage.
" Okay, I'll see what I can do." Suzan then kissed her mother and went to find the doctor. A tired smile crept upon Estelle's face.   "
Estelle what are you smiling about?" Charmaine asked as she sat in Suzan's place.
" After all these years, I'm finally going to be with John again. How I have waited for the moment to be reunited with him."
Suzan came back into the room. " Mum, I've spoken with the doctor, and he said it would be okay for you to go in the morning. He is arranging and ambulance and a wheelchair." With the wonderful news Suzan brought Estelle felt a calming relief touch her heart.
" It's getting quite late, so we'll all be back and see you in the morning." Suzan, Charmaine and Keith kissed Estelle goodnight and left the hospital.

That night Estelle could feel the calmness of death flow through her and fill her dreams of wondrous things, but the one thing she would remember is the sight of her husband. Estelle could feel the love and warmth of her loved one and the place where she walked.

" Estelle." A voice floated among the mist that surrounded her. " Estelle." The voice echoed, this time much clearer.   " John, is it you?" Estelle called and reaching out. As she did, she noticed something different, for her hands were the hands of a young woman, a warm breeze gently touched the white gown she wore.
" Hello Estelle, I've been waiting a long time for this moment."
" John?" Estelle looked up, " Oh John my love."   The two beings embraced and then gazed into each other's eyes. John took Estelle by the hand. " Come with me, I have something to show you." And then both walked down a stone path. A few moments past, then like the flick of a switch a light of brilliance filled the darkness, and all was revealed, for they stood in a field of flowers that shone with such a brilliance of colours." Estelle, my angel, this is where I will greet you tomorrow." He explained.
" John, this seems so real."
" My angel this is real, you can touch them too. This may not be earth, but everything is as real here as it is there."
" If this isn't earth, where are we?" Estelle questioned.
" This place is known as Paradise. It's a place where there is no pain, no suffering or illness, it's where the spirit comes to rest before its journey home. It's time for you to go now, our daughter is coming for you."

Estelle opened her eyes to the sound of her daughter's voice. " Well mum, today is the day you will see the field." The nurses helped Estelle into the ambulance

and loaded the wheelchair into the back.
" Aunt Charmaine, can you take the children I would like
to go with mum."
" Of course, Keith and I will follow behind."

The two vehicles made their way to the edge of the field,
where the flowers grew wild and in a rainbow of
magnificent colours. Estelle's heart filled with joy as she
knew it would not be long before she was to be reunited
with the ones she loved and longed for. They gently
lifted Estelle from the ambulance and into the
wheelchair. The wind was cold and bitter but scented
with the aroma of the flowers that lay before her.
" Here mum, have this." Suzan then tucked a woollen
rug around her mother's legs.
" Thank you dear, thank you so much for everything."
Estelle said looking up to her daughter.
" Oh mum. I love you so, so much and I know I could
have told you more often."
" I know my darling, it's alright. Is Charmaine here?"
" Yeah, I'll get her." Suzan then kissed her mother."
" Charmaine, I'm so happy you came, I could not have
asked for a better big sister, give me a hug."
Charmaine bent down to the chair and gave Estelle a
hug she could never forget.
" I love you Estelle, I'm going to miss you." Charmaine
then began to cry.
" Okay, I'm ready. Take me to the field." Estelle gently
spoke. Suzan, Charmaine, Keith, Billy and Jenny
walked with the ambulance driver as he pushed the
wheelchair into the middle of the field of flowers. As the
breeze blew Estelle could feel her freedom come
closer. The frail bodied woman sat in the field
surrounded by the beauty she loved. Some of the petals
were picked up by the winter breeze and danced around

her showering her with their beautiful aromas, dark clouds of snow began to fill the sky. Estelle opened her withered hand to catch the first snowflake as she did many times as a child, but for this was to be the last time. As the snowflake fell and came to rest upon her hand, so to would she breathe her last breath that would give her life.

A hush had fallen around them as a brilliant ray of light cut through the cloud lit up the field where the family stood filling them with the warmth it gave. Suzan looked through the brightness at a figure standing before her, she wiped the tears from her eyes to focus and standing there was her father. No words were spoken he simply smiled and took Estelle by the hand as she stood up from the wheelchair. Both spirits looked to Suzan and blew her a kiss then turned and walked off in the field, and as quick as it came the golden ray of light was gone and Estelle and John were once again united for all time and eternity.

THE END.

Book 2

The Sphere
Of
Eternal Life.

Chapter 1

" Good morning, Professor Brook, Professor Wade, is everything set?" I questioned.
" I think I have everything." answered Brook.
" Good, let's get going then. Time waits for no one." I said as I smiled. We loaded everything onto the van and started off for the airport. " What happened to Professor Slade and Ali?" enquired Wade.
" Oh, they said they'd meet up with us at the airport." I replied as I looked to him in the rear-view mirror. As we arrived at the airport Professor Wade and his assistant Ali were waiting for us at the main entrance. I pulled into the drop off zone and we unloaded everything out of the van onto baggage trolleys. After parking the van, I made my way to the others and we all checked in, collected our passes and made our way through security and boarded the plane. Making ourselves comfortable and ready for take-off the flight attendant announced a twenty-minute delay as there was slight traffic build up on the tarmac. We eventually left Sydney airport and began our journey for Buenos Aires where we were to catch another plane.

After sixteen hours in the air we finally landed in Buenos Aires where we had a three hour wait for our next flight. So, being the curious bunch, we are Professor Brook,

Wade and I hired a car and headed into the city while Professor Slade and Ali decided to stay at the airport. We pulled into a market area a short walk to the city centre. The market was a bustling place with stalls of all kinds, selling artefacts, locally made items and different types of foods. Brook and Wade went in one direction, and I headed off in the other. " We'll meet back at the car in one hour!" I yelled back to them.

Several minutes had passed since we split up and I felt myself being immersed into the surroundings of the market with the smells of exotic foods. Something had caught my attention and stopped me in my tracks. It was the feeling someone was following me, so I turned to see but no one was there so I kept walking. Still with the feel of someone there I turned the corner and hid behind a paling fence. I stood there for a moment looking between the gaps in the fence to try see this person, but still nothing. The I was grabbed from behind, a hand over my mouth and my arm was pulled back. " Stop," I begged, " You're hurting me." Then the stranger spoke in a deep husky voice, with a Russian accent. " Good, then you know I'm serious. You and your friends had better stop your journey, if you don't you will not be so lucky next time." He had let go of my arm and mouth and pushed me into the wall. I turned to see who it was, but he had vanished.

I straightened myself up and started my way back to the car looking around at everything and everyone as I went. I could hear footsteps behind me, so I picked up the pace and went faster. Still hearing them I began to run, I could see the car, so I turned to see who was behind me and in doing so I ran into someone. I struggled to break free of his hold, he pulled me closer and repeated. " Hey, calm down, calm down." I looked up and saw it was Professor Wade. " What is it? What's wrong?" He spoke in a concerned voice. " We must go, someone knows we are here and what we are looking for." I puffed out between breaths. The three of us got into the car and headed for the airport. We arrived at the airport ten minutes later to find Professor Slade and Ali nowhere to be seen, we looked around for a moment and then a messenger showed up and told us the two had already boarded the plane and are waiting for us. We took our seats and prepared for take-off.

As the plane started moving, I took a deep breath and slowly let it out, Professor Brook touched my hand and spoke. " Everything should be fine now," in a deep calming voice. Three hours later we landed in Rio De Janeiro and all five of us collected our equipment and baggage and walked to a private hanger for our charted flight to Manaus. We put our gear down outside the office and Slade went in to see if our plane was ready. He returned to us fifteen minutes later and spoke. " Well, I have some bad news. It seems our plane won't be ready for at least two days." " This is bullshit." Brook kicked one of his bags, " we were told it would be on time and no delays." So again, we picked up out bags and made our way to the Lynx Hotel that was situated near the airport. We all made our way up to rooms on the third floor taking three rooms on the floor. Professor Wade and Brook at the start of the floor, Slade and Ali at the other end and my room in the middle. All those hours of traveling I was desperate for a hot shower.

I entered my room and just dropped everything beside the bed, such a relief to see a bed and to look out a window where nothing was moving. I turned and fell across the bed and just lay there a few moments relaxing and thinking of what the next few days would bring. I slowly dragged myself off the bed and opened a window as it was tremendously hot. I unpacked some clothes and went into the bathroom for a relieving shower; I turned on the taps and started to undress. As I was about to step into the cubical, I realised I didn't bring my brush, so I went back into the bedroom to get it.

I came back into the bathroom and opened the shower door and took a step in. Sitting in the corner of the cubicle was a Brazilian Wandering Spider considered the world's deadliest. I froze in place feeling my heartbeat louder and the pulse in my neck get stronger. The spider began to rear up in an attack stance; I slowly backed away and as I did the creature using its rear legs lunged forward and making itself appear larger. As I jumped back, I tripped on the shower cubicle edge and screamed as I hit the towel rack and landed on the floor. Out of nowhere Professor Wade came running in, I pointed to the spider and so he killed it and threw it out.

He turned to me and wrapped a towel around me and helped me to my feet. Pulling me close to his chest with his arms around me his breathing was soothing, and the strength of his arms was comforting.
" Better?" He asked as he held me tight.
" Much better, thank you. How the hell did that get in here?"
" I don't know, but something about this isn't right. First the encounter in Buenos Aires and now this, I'm starting to think you may be right, that someone is trying to stop us."

Wade went back to his room, and I cautiously finished my shower. Half an hour later I dressed and went out for a walk, as I really needed to get out of the room. On leaving the hotel I bumped into Professor Slade.
" Would you care to join me for some lunch?" he asked. I hesitated for a moment, smiled and said yes. We walked down the street a short way and came across an outdoor cafe rather quaint open-air tables with a kiosk style kitchen. We sat at a table and ordered some drinks and food. We sat there for a while drinking, Slade then put down his drink and placed his hand upon mine slightly looking down and said, " I think you are the most attractive woman I have ever had the pleasure of knowing." I choked a little on my drink and replied, " Ah; thank you. We'd ah, we'd better be getting back to the others, they'll be wondering where we are." I held my breath and let out a sigh and sculled the rest of my drink. We left the cafe and made our way back to the Hotel.

As we were crossing the driveway that led under the Hotel a car came racing out towards me, I froze as it came closer and Professor Slade yelled, " Look Out!" He ran towards me and pushed me out of its path we both landed in the garden next to the driveway. As the car sped around the corner we climbed out of the garden and dusted ourselves down.
" Sorry about that, are you ok?" he asked.
" Yes, I think so, just a bit scratched. What the hell is it with people trying to kill me." I replied as I kept brushing off the dirt.

I went up to my room to get a fresh change of clothes Professor Brook and Wade came into my room.
" We just heard, what happened?" Brook asked with

concern. " Someone is trying to stop this expedition."
Wade said as he sat on the edge of the bed. Ali then
came into the room and asked, "How is everything
going?" We all turned and looked at him like he was
stupid. He then said as looked at me, " What the hell
happened to you? You look like you got pulled through a
hedge backwards."
" I was almost run down by a car." I pulled a twig out of
my hair.
" Are you ok? Did you get a good look at the driver?" he
questioned me.
" No, it was going too fast, it's kind of like a blur."
" Anyway, whoever it is, they are trying to stop us from
finding the sphere." Wade said standing up.

Ali then left the room and Wade watched through a
crack in the partially door to see Ali go back to his room.
" Well, I think we all better get some sleep." I suggested.
So, the two Professors went back to their rooms, and I
sat on a chair looking out of my room to the street below
trying to figure out who or why these things were
happening.

I climbed into bed and eventually drifted off to
sleep. The night air was so hot and heavy through the
night I threw off the sheet as it was too much to have
anything on me. As I rolled to the other side of the bed I
heard a noise on the balcony outside my room. " Is
somebody there?" I called out. I waited for an answer
but there was only silence, so I tried to go back to sleep. I
then heard the sliding door in the living room open, so I
took hold of the vase beside the bed and crept into the
living room. I couldn't see anything, so I closed the
doors and went back to bed. Almost asleep I was
disturbed by another noise, this time it was in the

bedroom, through the haziness of sleep I could see a
figure standing over me. He pulled out a gun, my eyes
widened as he came closer, as I rolled out of the way, the
gun fired, he missed and ran out of the room.

Professor Brook, Wade and Slade came running into the
room. With some tears and sweat running down my
face I sat up and pointed to the door. " He; he ran out
into the hall." Brook and Slade both ran out into the hall
to look for the intruder, and Wade went into the
bathroom and brought me a glass of water.
" Here, drink this." He quietly spoke.
" Thank you." I began to sip the water.

A few moments later the two Professors returned.
" Brook, Slade, ah you both better get some sleep, I think
I'll sleep on the lounge in case our stalker tries again."
Instructed Wade.

Morning came, and I got myself out of bed and ordered
breakfast for myself and Wade. After breakfast we all
met in the Hotel Lobby and when to the airport for our
plane. Professor Slade went into the office to check on
the progress of our plane, and it was ready. We loaded
our equipment and language onto the plane and took or
seats. The pilot started the engines, and we lifted off for
our next stop, Manaus.

Chapter 2

After four hours of flying, we landed in Manaus. As soon as we were off the plane, we found a small seaplane to hire to take us to Careiro, or at least to Pousada Mamori where we could get a room to freshen up, so we can continue our journey to Careiro.

So, after a thrilling two-hour flight we reached Pousada Mamori and looked forward to a shower wasn't bad for a three-star residence but at this stage I didn't really care I just wanted running water. The heat was really getting to us all and the humidity was heavy, but we knew we couldn't stop we had to push on.

A few hours had passed and all of us had freshened up and as much as the thought of sleeping was overwhelming, we just couldn't until we reached Careiro. Professor Slade headed out to find us suitable transport to get us the rest of the way while Brook, Wade, Ali and I check the equipment to make sure all was in order.
" Ok, I found us something." Slade announced as he walked into the room. " It's not much but they said it'll get us to Careiro."
" What is it?" Brook asked.
" Ah, it's a van, but it's sturdy and the tyres look good."
Brook, Wade and I looked at each other giving the " Oh Shit" look. We picked up everything and when down to load up this van and as we got outside, we stopped dead

in our tracks, out of shock I dropped the bags. What was presented to us was almost hard to describe. Yes, it was a van once upon a time, two back windows were missing, the bonnet looked like an elephant had sat on it, the front passenger door was not there, and the side doors were half cut off, but yes, the tyres were good, sturdy? that's yet to be seen.

" Well, I guess we better load up and get started." Professor Brook said walking towards the van. We pried open the rear door and loaded everything in, Wade and Brook up front and me, Slade and Ali in the back. After a few attempts at starting our clapped-out transport and with an explosion of smoke out the exhaust we were finally on our way to Careiro. After an hour or so and on the road from hell we finally reached Careiro and went straight to a hotel as night was falling and rest was a major priority. After settling into our rooms, we all headed down to the bar for food and something cold to drink. We all sat out in the beer garden in the cool night air, eating, drinking and listening to the music a local band was playing and the crickets in the background seemed to be in time with the band, so I went inside to get another round for the table.

As I was at the bar waiting, one of the locals decided I was lonely and needed company, I ignored him at first, so he tried again. " Hey baby, how's about a drink." He mumbled through his drunken breath.
" No, thank you. I'm quite capable of buying my own."
" Ok, then why don't you show me a good time, and we can have some fun." He continued to dribble on.
" Listen fatso, what part of NO don't you understand."
He then grabbed my arm and spun me around, and as I came around, I slapped him. He looked back at me,

" Bitch." Then with full force punched me in the jaw. I yelled and fell back onto the bar, and he came at me again, so I grabbed a bottle from beside me and belted him with it to the side of the head, he fell to the floor. I turned and tried to walk away, as I did, he grabbed my foot and tripped me. I tried to crawl away, and he took hold of my ankle and started to pull me towards him, I turned over and started kicking him in the face.
" Wade! Brook!" I screamed. This man was like he was possessed, blood gushed from his head and nose. I screamed again. Professor Wade and Brook ran in and pulled the guy off me, then Slade came in and helped me off the floor. Wade and Brook threw the drunk out of the Hotel.
" You're bleeding." said Slade and he wiped the blood from my mouth. Brook and Wade came back into the bar.
" What the hell happened to that guy?" Brook asked.
" Oh, I hit him with a bottle."
" Shit, I'd hate to meet you in a dark alley." Wade said jokingly. We all looked at each other and laughed.

Morning crept into my room; I could feel the sun's rays warming my cool skin as the nights were rather cool in the Amazon region. I rolled over to look at the bedside clock, there was three hours till we were to catch the boat to Parintins, so I dragged myself out of bed and showered and went to meet the others for breakfast. Professor Brook greeted me with a kiss and Ali came around pull my chair out for me. " Thank you, Ali." Then we all ordered breakfast. The kitchen hand brought out the orders on a large tray and for some reason mine was covered. Just as we were about to start, I slowly lifted the cover off mine to see if there was anything strange in place of my order, and with a calming sigh of relief it was

exactly what I wanted, so we started to eat. It was a feast
fit for kings, upon finishing we collected our belongings
and equipment as time was getting away from us, so we
met in the bar for one last drink before setting off on our
journey.

" Wade, Brook." I yelled, " Where the hell is Slade and
Ali?"
" They left a message they'll meet us at the boat." Wade
replied.
" Well then gentlemen, what are we waiting for. Let's get
going." I said then throwing down the last of my drink.
We reached the boat with the sight of Slade and Ali
loading everything on board. After securing the
equipment we set off down river to Parintins.

The air was quite hot and humid, we have now been on
the river ten hours, one of our guides leaned over the
edge of the boat splashing water on his face. Hurling out
of nowhere a spear pierced the deck beside me, I
screamed and lept to Professor Wade. Then the guide
leaning over the edge of the boat was dragged into the
river, Brook dove for his feet but was too late. Two of the
crew members pulled out some rifles and started
shooting into the thick bush that lined the river, Ali ran
over and took me into the wheelhouse, spears were
flying in all directions.

" Please, you must stay here. You will be much safer." Ali
said as he sat me in the corner. Ali ran back out on deck,
and more rifles were brought out. I then crept over to a
window and slowly stood up, and as I did a spear came
flying past my head, so I stood up a bit higher and as I
did a black face popped up with mine, we stared for a
moment and then I screamed, and he screamed but he

was louder so with full force I landed a punch to his nose knocking him off the boat. " Screw this shit." I mumbled to myself, so I pulled the spear out of the cabin wall and threw it back to where it came from. Tribesmen were beginning to climb onto the boat, so I searched through the wheelhouse to find a gun, it was like watching a small battle. I had almost given up searching when I could hear the floorboards creaking behind me, and it was getting closer. I finally came across and handgun, I spun around and started shooting at him unfortunately missing every time. I eventually ran out of bullets, so I then threw it at him and still I bloody missed him. As he came closer, he pulled out a rather large knife, I looked around for something, anything to fend him off and there was a club by the boats wheel, I picked it up and started swinging like a crazy woman. He bobbed left and right and with one last mighty swing I closed my eyes and went for it, hearing a thump I opened my eyes and saw what I did. " I got him! I got him!" I shouted and then everything went black.

A few moments later I awoke with a slap to my cheek, I opened my eyes, pushed the person out of the way and jumped to my feet. " It's ok," said Brook, " It's all over." " It is?" I replied slightly confused, " What happened?" " When Slade and Ali came in after we cleared the boat, they found you and your friend you clobbered lying on the floor, and so here we are now." Brook explained. " We still have a five-hour boat ride on this bloody river, so we better eat and get some rest." Suggested Professor Wade as he stood in the doorway.

I woke about an hour or so later, walked to the stern of the boat. A breeze began to blow, it felt so cool through my sweat dampened shirt, such a relief was welcome. As

I was enjoying the breeze I could hear footsteps behind me, so I turned to see who was there. On turning I slipped and heard a gunshot, it was one of the natives, he must have been hiding onboard, he fell against me and I went flying off the boat into the river. I started to scream out for help, I could see alligators slide into the river's edge, I screamed out again for help. Wade and brook came running to the edge of the boat, Brook threw in a life ring and Wade dove in and started swimming towards me. " Try and stay calm." Brook yelled. Wade finally reached me and place my arms around his neck and asked, " Are you ok? relax and let me do the work." There was no way I was going to argue with that I was stuffed and well as long as Wade had hold of me, I couldn't be any happier. " Ah, I've been better." I breathlessly replied. " As nice as this is we had better get back to the boat or we might just be snacks." We reached the boat, Brook and Slade helped us back onboard and Ali handed us towels.

We finally reached the docks of Parintins, the dock hands unloaded our equipment, and we headed off to the hotel to clean up. I looked out of the dingy windows in my room, with the air still thick and humid clouds were brewing up.
" Oh great, that's all I need, a bloody rainstorm." I quietly mumbled. So, I pulled the shutters closed and went to see Wade.

I stood outside his door for a moment then continued to knock.
" Come in."
" It seems we're in for a bit of a washdown." I said walking toward a window.
" Well, I guess this means we'll be stuck in this heavenly

hole." Wade said as he smiled.
" Come on, let's get the other two and get some dinner."
Brook said. So, we collected Slade and Ali and went
down to see what we could find. That moment the skies
opened, and the rain fell, harder by the minute.

We sat at a table in the middle of the room with drinks
in hand waiting for food to arrive, and with a clap of
thunder the roof opened, and a flow of water poured in.
Drenched we sat there looking at each other.
" Oh great," said Slade, " What else could happen."
" Well, we could be stuck here for days." I said wiping
water from my face.
" Don't say that you'll give us all bad luck." Ali said.
So, we all looked at each other and just laughed.
" Come on, we better move or we'll all end up sick as
dogs." suggested Wade. We all moved over to the bar
where it was somewhat dryer.
" Hey bartender, when do you think the rain will stop?"
asked Brook.
" Well, maybe tomorrow, maybe the day after, maybe
next week, who knows."
" Well, we better make ourselves comfortable." said
Wade.

Two nights had passed, and the rain kept on falling. The
third day came, and the morning was clear, such a relief
to see the sun. So, I got out of bed and dressed and down
the hall to see Wade, so we may discuss the journey
ahead. As I entered the room Professor Wade was still
dressing.
" Take a seat, I won't be long." he yelled out from the
bathroom. As I sat on a chair in the corner of the room, I
caught his reflection in a mirror that was on the wall
opposite the bathroom. I could see his olive toned skin

reflecting the morning sun off his well-formed
chest. His body was smooth and unblemished, I could
feel myself blushing but couldn't resist watching.
" It's a good change in the weather isn't it." With my
mind elsewhere I answered, " Oh, just beautiful." As he
came out of the bathroom his torso caught the fullness
of the sunlight, I'm sure my jaw hit the floor. As our eyes
met, I felt myself blush even more, so I quickly looked to
the window next to me.

He came towards me and placed his shirt on the bed
next to me. As he took my hand I rose from the chair, we
gazed into each other's eyes for a moment, I took a deep
breath and pressed my lips together. He took me in his
arms, our lips touched, his lips were tender and warm. I
could feel his strength, his heart beating next to mine,
the smell of his skin was bewildering. We stopped and
just held each other for a minute. " How I've waited for
this moment." Wade quietly spoke.

Once again, we looked into each other's eyes, I smiled,
and we started to kiss again, I felt giddy from the
sensation. He started to unbutton my shirt and slowly
slid it from my shoulders. Gravity didn't exist as we
floated back onto the bed, a deep sigh escaped my lips as
he kissed around my neck, slowly and gently moving
down between my breasts, I could feel my body
surrendering. I placed my hands upon the back of his
neck and slowly ran them down his strong smooth back;
the sound of my pulse was almost deafening as it beat
uncontrollable in my head and through my hands I
could feel his beating in time with mine. The air in the
room grew warmer and sweat began to drip from our
bodies. He kissed his way down to my navel rolling his
tongue as he went. He carefully slid my underwear down

my legs continuing to kiss his way down the rest of my body. He crawled his way back up my body like a lion stalking his prey. Our lips met with fiery passion his tongue was hot and wet, his gentle but firm hands gripped my waist as he pulled me into his body, I could feel him inside of me, my back arched and sweat ran from my breasts and the sun reflecting from the beads of sweat that sat upon his chest. We became one reaching the climax of passion, his body tensing with every motion. With the power I felt I was pulled upright against his chest as both our bodies shuddered with the explosion we felt. Exhausted we both fell back to the bed and lay there and drifted off to sleep.

As I woke, I watch him lay there with the sun lighting up the muscular lines of his body. I moved his hair with my fingers and softly ran them down the middle of his back trying not to wake him. He then rolled over opened his eyes and smiled. We leaned to each other and kissed. " Hi." he spoke in a whisper.
" I think we had better make a move or we will be running behind time." I said kissing him again. He rose out of bed and so I watched him dress.
" You can get a good view from this angle." I said with a small laugh. After I finished dressing, I went back to my room to pack my things ready for the rest of the journey. As I was packing there was a knock at the door.
" Are you ready to load everything on the boat?" It was Ali.
" Just about. I've got a few more things to do." I answered. " Ali, tell everyone we'll meet in the bar before leaving."
" Will do." he replied. I finished packing and went to the door, as I was about to open it there was another knock on the door. " Just a minute." I yelled out as I dropped

all my bags. I continued to open the door, but no one was there and as I turned, I saw a note stuck to the door with a knife, and it said.

" I warned you before to stop your journey, NOW! I'm tell you. everywhere you go, every move you make, I will be watching. I am never far away so watch your back!"

I then ran back into the room and grabbed everything and got down to the bar.
" Guys, we've got a problem. He's here, he's followed us here." I yelled as I ran into the bar.
" What's wrong? Who's here?" asked Wade.
" The guy I told you about, the one that grabbed me in Rio." I handed Wade the note. He read it and then handed it to Brook.
" Well then, I guess we better get a head start and make a move." Brook said as he handed the message back to me.

So, we picked up all the equipment and made our way to the boat. Ali then took the note from my hand and said, " I'll look after the note, so we can study it later." Halfway between Parintins and Faro we stopped to take a quick dip to cool down as the heat was getting unbearable. While swimming I could see Ali and Professor Slade walk off into the forest, so out of curiosity I decided to follow.
" Where are you going?" yelled Brook.
" Nowhere, just going to stretch my legs."
" Watch out for snakes and spiders." Wade warned.
" No worries, I'll watch out for the little creepy crawlies." I smartly answered.

I continued to follow Slade and Ali into the forest; I eventually got them in my sights. I couldn't quite hear what they were saying, so I tried to get as close as I possibly could without making a sound, as I did, I stepped onto a dead twig. They immediately stopped talking. I quickly dropped to my knees behind a small thicket, fortunately they did not see me, so they kept on talking.

" Now Ali, remember the deal." Slade said.
" Yeah sure, I take out Brook and Wade and. "
" Yeah, and I take care of the rest." Slade cutting him off.

In shock of what I heard, on my hands and knees I crawled as fast as I could. Cutting my knees, I eventually got to my feet and started running looking behind me as I went. Coming out of the forest I started yelling, "
Wade. Brook. I just."
" Hey, what's the problem?" Slade asked. At the shock of hearing him I stopped dead and took a deep breath, "
Ah. ah. I saw a snake, yeah that's it a snake a real big snake."
" Well, I guess we wasted enough time; we had better make a move." suggested Wade. We loaded a few things back onto the boat and continued up the waterway leading to our final destination.

Night fall came, and the mosquitoes were getting very bad and very big, so we sprayed each other with insect repellent. As the night went on, I could see Wade standing at the front of the boat looking up at the stars.
" Hi there." I said as I stood beside him.
" Nice aren't they, the stars, don't you think, they shine like your eyes in the midday sun." he whispered.
" Oh, you can do better than that can't you." I said

raising an eyebrow.

" Well, I could, but there are too many people on the boat." he replied giving a little laugh.

"Well, that's a good enough excuse, but next time you won't get away with it." I said with a smile, " I'm turning in it's going to be a long day tomorrow." I turned and walked off to the cabin.

As the warmth of the morning sun crept across my face, I opened my left eye to see where it was coming from, and as I could see the window I decided to roll over, I disgust and tried to go back to sleep. Then as I did, I was thrown out of bed and onto the floor. Holding my head from the impact, I crawled up to the window to see what the hell was going on. " Are you ok?" Ali asked as he came running into the room.

" Bloody marvellous." I snapped at him. " I just love being thrown out onto the floor first thing in the morning." Holding my head, I added, " What the hell happened?"

" The boat ran aground." He explained.

" What bloody idiot did that?"

" Never mind that, we've got to get all the equipment off the boat!"

" Well, where's the others?" I questioned.

" Professor Wade and Professor Brook are trying to stop the boat from sinking." he explained.

" Fine, ok, go and help Slade and I'll collect my notes and whatever else I can carry." I said as I ordered him to go. I quickly gathered all my notes, belongings and what equipment and dashed out to the boat's edge and started throwing what I could onto the riverbank. Wade came from below deck carrying cases of equipment; Brook wasn't far behind. " The boat can't be saved the hull is completely ripped open." Wade explained as he jumped into the water.

The boat began to creak and moan as it filled with water and tipping to one side, Brook jumped into the water with what he could carry, but no sign of Slade and Ali. Brook and Wade made their way to the riverbank dragging with then what they could manage.
" Where the hell is Slade and Ali?" Wade yelled.
" We can't wait any longer, I'll go in and get them." I threw to the bank what I had and went back to the boat.
" We're going to have to leave the boat and walk the rest of the way!" Brook hollered. I reboarded the boat and went below deck to find them.
" Slade! Ali! Get the hell out of there, it's about to go under!"

At that moment the boat came adrift and began to rapidly descend beneath the river surface. The water was rising so fast we were running out of breathing space. The boat started to cave in, and timber was falling around us. I dove off the stairwell to help the other two get out before the boat was fully submerged. It was too late the boat had hit the bottom of the river, planks of wood were being tossed around from the rushing water and as I turned, I was struck with a beam and was knocked to the bottom. Struggling to free my legs from beneath the beam I looked around and saw Brook coming towards me. He gestured with his hands to what he was going to do, so I braced myself for the release of pressure. After a few attempts he managed to lift the beam and free my legs. I could feel myself losing consciousness Brook my face in his hands placed his mouth over mine, I could feel the air he gave me fill my lungs, so I gave him a thumbs up and we swam to the top. As we burst through river surface and the change of pressure we both let out a loud gasp for fresh air. Wade dived in and helped Brook and me back to the riverbank.

Heaving for air Wade and Brook laid me out on the bank to rest and catch my breath. Wade tore open the legs of my pants to assess the wound.
" Well, it isn't too bad. The skins a bit broken and there's some bad bruising, but I guess you'll live."
" Thank you, Doctor Wade. Thank you for your concern.

Chapter 3

Looking at the map I announced, " Looks like it's going to be at least a two-day hike north to Faro, so we should get started." The few crew members from the boat and the five of us picked up all the equipment and we started off on our trek. " Do you think you can walk that far?" Slade asked.
" Don't you worry about it; I can keep up with you guys."

We walked on for a several hours, the air starts to slightly cool down as the afternoon went on, insects were still a pain in the arse. We did our best to follow the waterway Wade then turned to me and asked, " Are you sure you don't need any help?"
" Don't worry, you'll be the first to know." I answered. Nightfall came, and we decided to make camp. Sitting in my tent looking through my notes, I discovered that the plans for the interior of the temple were missing, I had to find them as soon as possible.

" Wade, Brook, hurry!" I called. Seconds later the two Professors entered my tent.
" What's the problem?" Brook questioned.
" It's the plans for the temple, they're gone."
" Have you looked everywhere?" Wade interrupted.
" Yes, of course," I snapped at him. " Sorry, it just frightens me that they could fall into the wrong hands. It could mean widespread devastation."
Looking worried Wade asked, " Who do think took

them?" Taking a deep breath, I said, " I have my suspicion, but I can't be certain yet but I'm pretty sure."
" Well, don't keep us in suspense." Brook said anxiously.

" Well, I wasn't sure when to tell you both this, but I think now's a better time than any," I paused. " Do you remember when we stopped the boat a few hours after we left Parintins to cool off in the river."
" Yeah." interrupted Brook.
"Well, I followed Slade and Ali into the forest and heard them talking. It sounded like they were making plans to double cross us for the sphere, I don't know if they are responsible for the threats, but they may have the plans, but I'm still not sure how they would have got their hands on them."
" Ali might have taken it when we ran aground as I left him for a moment to organise the equipment." Wade suggested.
" No, it couldn't have been him, he was helping me as we hit the sandbar. Did you see where Slade was?" I said trying to remember.
" Come to think of it, no." Brook said.
" Hmm, we'll just have to watch them, or this expedition could end in the biggest tragedy ever." I said trying my best to keep my voice down. " Well, I think we will call it a night, we've got an early start tomorrow."
" Yeah, well goodnight and see you both at dawn." Brook said as he walked out of the tent. Wade knelt before me and said, "We'd ah, better take a look at your ankle."
" If you must."
" Well then swelling has eased, and the bruising has gone, but the rest of your leg looks great." he commented.
" Thank you for your time, but I think we'll finish the consultation." Wade stood up and gently kissed me then

placing his hands to either side of my face whispered, " Goodnight."

Morning came, and the crew were packing the camping gear and tents.
" Good morning, Slade and Ali, isn't it a beautiful day." I said as I tied my hair back.
" Isn't it just." Ali replied.
" What was all the commotion last night." Slade asked.
" Oh nothing, I thought I saw a spider."
" Well as long as it wasn't too serious." Slade said as he picked up his backpack. Everything was eventually packed, and we hit the trail to continue the trek to Faro. As we walked through the forest, I could hear Howler Monkeys. Their call echoed through the forest and got louder as we approached their territory, so I paused to look around and Then I saw a family of them in the trees above, calling to one another of our approach warning others of the strangers in their jungle.
" Wade!" I tried to call quietly.
" What is it." " Bring me a camera, I want to get a shot of the monkeys." As he handed me the camera I smiled and said, " Be a honey and take the shot for me, it's a bit hard balancing on one ankle." I said looking sorry for myself as I motioned with my sore ankle.
" Well,' since you put it that way, how can I refuse." After taking a few shots we started moving on. The day grew hotter and more humid and the jungle a little thicker. More monkeys could be seen in the treetops and their eyes following our journey as though they were keeping check on us. The sun was descending as we entered late afternoon and the sounds of the night creatures began to stir.
" Brook, do you think we should camp here for the night?" I asked in a suggestive way.

" I guess we could, your ankle still needs to fully heal." Brook let out a loud whistle to signal for the party to stop. After twelve hours trekking on a screwed-up ankle it was a relief to sit, the site was a hive of activity as tents were being raised and campfires built.

The songs of the birds of the jungle sang out that morning and the warmth of the sun could be felt already, wade brought me in coffee, the aroma filled my tent.
" Good morning. Thought you might like a little kick start."
" Mm smells wonderful. Thank you."
" Well, only a few hours to go before we reach Faro. Most of the site is packed and ready to go." Wade brushed my hair from my face. After packing, the party heading off for the last stretch to Faro, just the thought of hot running water was bliss.
" So, guys, what is everyone going to do first when we reach Faro?" I yelled out.
" I intend to have a long soak in a tub." Proclaimed Wade.
" And what will you be doing Slade?" I yelled from the end of the line. Turning as he walked Slade answered, " Finding a place for a stiff drink."

We reached Faro Inn. It was only a small place but comfortable enough, well five-star luxury compared to a tent. Brook, Wade and I went into the Inn, Slade and Ali went straight to the bar. I entered my room and had a look around, " Oh hell." I thought to myself in disgust. There were a small sink and dingy old mirror next to the window and half a curtain that looked like a giant moth had eaten, but still better than a tent. I threw my gear on the bed and went to wash my face and hands before eating. I stood for a moment looking into the mirror, " You look like shit." I mumbled to my reflection. Then I washed my face and hands and attempted to rake my hair. " Hmm, slight improvement." Again, I mumbled to myself. I met the others down in the bar to get something to eat.

Wade and I went for a bit of a walk down the main street, it wasn't much wider than a dirt track still muddy from the previous rain. We walked past the bar Slade and Ali went in, we could hear some kind of commotion, so we stopped and looked in.
" Should've known who the imbeciles were that would have started something like this." stated Wade.
" Well, do you think we should give them a hand." I said raising and eyebrow.
" Nah, let them sweat a bit longer."
" I like the way you think Professor Wade." We went into the bar and sat in the corner watching, bottles and chairs were flying in all directions.
" Now do you think?" I asked.
" A couple of more minutes won't hurt. "Wade replied. Then at that moment a chair came hurling towards us.
" Oh shit!" I yelled. In that instance we had dived onto the floor and crawled under the table and looked at each other.
" Now, can we?" I asked.
" Let's go for it." We got out from under the table and went for the crowd at the bar. I picked up a bottle that was on a table and ran to a guy that was about to hit Ali, I tapped the guy on the shoulder and said, " Excuse me." He turned and smiled so I smiled back and then hit him with the bottle.
" Thanks." Ali said gratefully. We turned and kept on fighting, I ran to the other end of the bar, Slade was

pinned down by two guys to the edge of the bar and a third about to lay into him, so I grabbed the third guy by his collar and dragged him off Slade throwing him to the floor. I helped Slade off the counter and to his feet.

" Look out!" Slade yelled. I turned and saw the guy that was on the floor had got up and started to swing a chair at us, we ducked, and the chair broke above us.
" You son of a bitch." I mumbled as I jumped to my feet, I slugged him as hard as I could. " That'll teach you to mess with a woman." I said to him as he hit the floor. I looked over to Wade he was getting stuck into by a few fellers, so I picked up the leg of a chair and started to belt my way through. Swinging in all directions bodies were flying and landing everywhere. I eventually got through them all, puffing and panting I stood there smiling at Wade.
" Behind you!" Wade yelled. I turned and swung the chair leg with all my strength and knocked the guy over the bar and into the shelving. The fight was over, Wade and the others got up from the floor. I went to the barman and put my hand in my pocket, he put his hands over his face and said, " Please don't hit me I do nothing."
" Don't worry, I just want to pay for damages." I said then handing over money. " Come on," I said looking at everyone, " Let's get back to the hotel and get cleaned up, and no more booze you two." I said looking at Slade and Ali. We dragged ourselves back to the hotel and to our rooms, If I wasn't exhausted before I am now but at the same time invigorated.

Morning came, and my body felt as though I had been run over several times. I slightly opened my eyes sat up and looked around the room, placed my hand to my head to cradle the throbbing, leaning to the edge of the bed I lost my balance and fell to the floor with a rather hard thump.   " Oh hell." I mumbled as I picked my face up off the floor. I slowly packed and gathered everything, I pulled out some fresh clothes and went into the bathroom and turned on the shower. Just as I was about to step in there was a knock at the door, so I grabbed a towel and wrapped it around me. I ran through the room clinging onto the towel and balancing myself by using the furniture, the knocking continued. " I'm coming!" I yelled. Then I reached for the door and opened it, but there was not a person to be seen, so I stuck my head out of the door and yelled down the corridor, " Dickhead." I slammed the door and went back to the shower. I stood there in the steam filled cubicle soaking up the hot water, after about fifteen minutes I decided to get out. As I was drying myself, I could hear someone in the next room, quickly I put on my shirt and grabbed the shower brush, being made of wood I thought it would make the biggest impact.

As the person came closer to the bathroom I stood behind the door and held the brush above my head at the ready, as the door slowly crept open I took a deep breath, closed my eyes and swung as hard as I could, the body hit the floor. Opening one eye I saw it was Wade.
" Wade!" I yelled. I dropped the brush and started to gently slap his face to bring him round.
" Oh Wade, I'm sorry, wake up. Oh please." I begged as I kept on slapping.
" What the hell was that?" Wade started to fend off my slaps. " Oh, it was me. I hit you with the shower brush." I explained. " You ought to be registered as a lethal weapon." He started rubbing the back of his head. I

helped him off the floor and placed a cold washer to the back of his head.

" I only came to see if you were ok from all the excitement from last night." Wade said as he handed me the washer. " Well, as you can see, I'm quite fine, just a bit of a headache."
" I better let you finish; I don't wish to be smacked around again. I'll see you downstairs with the others."
" We're all ready to go and all equipment counted for." Brook was always on top of things.
" Well then. Let's get started." I spoke.

We started north for the Temple of the Sphere. After several hours of hiking the party stopped for a short break as we all needed to catch our breath as the heat was building and becoming unbearable.
" Brook, Wade, remember to keep an eye on Slade and Ali." I instructed. " They still have the plans for the temple."
" Shouldn't we make a move to get it back?" Brook asked.
" No, not as yet." Wade answered.
" Well, when then." Brook questioned further.
" When they least expect it." Wade said as he watched the two in question.
" We had better keep moving, there are still a few good hours of daylight left." I spoke. We picked up our gear and started off. " Move out!" yelled Brook. The members and the crew collected the equipment, and we headed further into the jungle.

As the day went on the late afternoon shadows began to stretch their reach across the canopy above. Being deep into the jungle nightfall came rather quickly, Wade and Brook came into my tent to discuss the journey ahead.

" Wade, we should reach the area of the last sighting of the Priestesses Village, hopefully in twenty-four hours." I said going through my notes and whatever maps I had left to go by. " As we enter perimeter of the area, we will have to keep an eye out for any signs or clues for directions to the sight." Brook continued to say.
" When we reach the village, we will have to search for ways to and around the temple since Slade and Ali have the plans." Wade added.
" Well, we better get some sleep, as we have a long trek ahead of us." I suggested. As Brook left the tent I stood up and held Wade back.
" Wade, we had better watch our step, as I feel Slade and Ali may try something, so please take care." I quietly spoke.
" Don't worry about me, I can take care of those two." Wade then kissed my hand and left the tent. I sat on my stretcher and laid back onto the pillow. As I started to drift off, I could hear the harmonious chorus of the howler monkeys in the distance along with the nocturnal birds of the night.

I awoke the next morning feeling the heat and hearing the raised voice of Wade. I quickly shot off the stretcher and ran out of my tent. " Wade!" I yelled, " What the hell is going on?"   " It's Slade and Ali." He answered.
" What about them?"
" The bloody idiots have taken off."
" When." I said as I ran my fingers through my tangled hair.
" I think sometime during the night, and it looks like they've taken some of the equipment and supplies."

" Shit, that means they could be halfway there, damn it! there's no time to waste, we have to get moving." I ran back into my tent and quickly bundled everything together and roughly packed it. The few crew we had left finished packing what equipment and supplies were left, and we headed deeper into the jungle.

We had now been hiking ten hours through the humid thick undergrowth of the jungle floor moisture dripped from the trees above us and sweat ran down our backs, and in our minds, we could sense prying eyes watching our every move, or maybe it was the heat play tricks with our minds. I stopped to turn to Brook and Wade, " Remember, keep an eye out for any signs, clues. Any markings on trees or on stones, something that will tell us we are going in the right direction to the village."

So, we split up into three lines, five meters apart moving quickly but carefully, examining every tree, rock and crevice we came across in hope that something might stand out. " Wade, have you found anything yet?" I called out.
" No, not a clue."
" Brook, what about you? anything?"
" Not as yet. Wait a minute, I think I just did. Come take a look, I think it's what we've been looking for." he yelled with some excitement. Wade and I ran to Brook as fast as we could. " Where is it?" I anxiously asked.
" Down here, it's buried in the ground." Brook said as he knelt and started brush away soil.

" Well, I never. A footstone in the shape of an arrowhead." Wade said as he helped Brook uncover the clue.
" Would it lead to the village you think?" Brook asked.

" Well, there's only one way to find out. We'll just have to continue in this direction and see where it takes us." I said as I took a picture. Brook took note of where we were and where the marker was on the trail, and we continued. Large boulders and remnants of a stone path were scattered along the tail we walked, one of the crew called out from where he stopped ahead. The two professors and I ran ahead to where the crewman stood, and there it was, a calving in a boulder covered by vines, a symbol that showed we were going in the right direction.
" Guys we must be careful where we step, for I have read that the villagers that protected the village set traps on all the paths leading in and out of the village, so please take care and keep an eye out." I took another picture of this marker and again Brook took note of its location.

I then turned and fell, Wade helped me to my feet and I brushed myself off.
" Are you ok, are you hurt?" Wade asked.
" No, I'm fine. What the hell did I trip over?"
" Well, as far as I can see it was this vine." Wade said as he picked it up to show me.

At that moment, the ground began to violently shake, the crew dropped everything and started running in all directions.
" What's happening!" I yelled.
" The vine you tripped over must be one of those traps you were telling us about." Brook yelled. As the vibrations were coming closer behind us, I turned to see what was causing it. Along the path we were on trees were falling in all directions and as they came closer to where we stood, I began to freeze. " What the hell are you waiting for." Wade shouted. " RUN!" He then

grabbed my arm and began running, dropping everything as I ran, I began to scream, " I'm gonna die! I'm gonna die! I don't wanna die I'm too young and pretty to die!"
" Will you just shut up and run!" Wade yelled.
" Ok!" I said as I wiped muddy tears from my face. We kept on running through the jungle to escape the falling trees, time was running out as they got closer and my life started to flash before my eyes, and as I hadn't done much it didn't take too long. " Look, there, a cave." Wade pointed out. The falling trees were almost upon us.
" We better bloody well hurry; those trees are falling faster and more of them." I bellowed as we changed direction. We Finally reached the cave, and as the trees stopped falling, they completely blocked the cave entrance.
" What are we going to do now?" I said trying to catch my breath. " Well, all we can do now is follow the cave and see if there's a way out." Wade stood there shining a torch into the darkness behind us.

Chapter 4

As we gazed into the dimly darkness of the cave, we could hear the echo of the rumbling from the falling trees. The air was slightly damp but at least we were out of the danger for now.

" We had better make a move I have not telling how long the batteries will last in this torch." Wade said turning the light to us. Some branches had fallen into the cave, so we used those as a means of keeping a circumference around us in case of any creatures that might live in the cave. Walking through tunnels drops of water could be heard as they echoed and large webs spread along the walls making the cave tunnels even creepier than before.

" How are you holding out?" Wade asked.

" Oh, I'm fine as long as I can't see what's in here, I'll be ok, but we need to try and move faster." I replied. We had been walking for close to an hour now and the tunnel started to get warmer as we went on.

" Wade, look. Is that a stairway?" I said as I walked ahead.

" Try not to touch anything, there may be a trap of some sort." cautioned Wade.

" You have nothing to worry about, I won't touch a thing, I promise." I said leaning against the wall.

" Well, we better get a move on if we wish to find Brook and the crew." he instructed.

" I can't wait to get my hands-on Slade and Ali when I

get out of here, I'll wring their bloody necks." I said walking towards Wade. As we took the first step on the stairwell the cave ground began to tremble.
" Now what's going on." I said looking around the cavern. " We must have set off another trap; I haven't touch anything did you?" Wade asked as he took my hand.
" I don't think so, all I did was lean against the wall." I took a step closer to him. We looked over at the wall to where I had stood to see what had been moved, a large stone had been pushed into the wall. " Woops." I said placing my arms around him. At that moment the ground beneath us opened up, Wade and I started falling, rocks and dirt came pouring in after us. I started to scream as I fell, " OH SHIT!"

We landed on the bottom of the cavity with dirt still falling like it was a waterfall, I quickly crawled under what I thought was a ledge. After a few moments the rocks and dirt stopped falling, I came out from the ledge and stood up.
" Wade!" I yelled, " Where are you?"
" Over here." His muffled voice made its way through the dust. " Are you ok? Do you still have the torch?" I dusted myself off.
"Yeah, it's right here."
" Ah. Well turn it on, I don't think I'm alone." I stood frozen not game to move and then the torch light made its way through the dust followed be Wade. I took a deep breath and slowly turned, uncertain of what I might see I closed my eyes and put out my hand. I could feel something quite lumpy, I moved my hand a little higher and opened my eyes, I slowly looked up. In shock of what it was I screamed and turned to run to wade, in doing so I fell against another skeleton.

" Wade! get over here!" I yelled, " I'm surrounded by
dead people!"

Wade ran over and pulled the skeletons away. " This
must be some kind of tomb." he said as he pulled me out
from the pile of bones. " I don't care what it is, I just
want to get out of this hell hole."
" Come on. This is no ordinary hole; it carries on a way."
he said as he took my hand. We made our way out of the
bone bin and carried on down a narrow passageway.
" Wade, have you noticed how the ground seems to
squelch with every step we take?" I questioned gripping
his hand tighter. " Strange isn't it." he said as he looked
back at me with a concerned look on his face. He
lowered the torch light to the floor; my eyes widened in
disgust. Cockroaches, centipedes, bugs of all kinds were
covering the ground. I screamed and pushed Wade out
of the way and started running, my voice echoing from
all directions.
" Hey!" he yelled, " Wait!"
I tripped and fell, " OH SHIT! Wade! get your arse down
here. I'm surrounded by cockroaches!" I screamed out as
they started to crawl onto my hands and into my hair.

I struggled to my feet and began throwing off the
roaches, I kept screaming for help and could see wade
running through the tunnel. Wade took off his hat and
started knocking off the roaches. " Ok, they're off. now
get moving." he ordered. We kept on moving down the
tunnel, a rush of air could be felt coming from behind us
and dust was filling the air and rumbling sound could be
heard. I turned to look behind us, and the ceiling was
caving in.
" Wade, I think I set off another trap." I yelled.
" Oh great!"

" What is it?" I asked.
" It's a dead end!"
" Great. No way out and we're about to be squashed." I
said as I placed my hands to the sides of my face.

" No, wait there just might be a way out." he said, " It
seems the Amazons left a helping hand." he turned and
showed me a panel of leavers.
" We better bloody hurry up and find the right leaver
we're running out of time."
" Then bloody well get over here and help me, you're the
expert." he yelled as he dragged me over. We started
going through the sequence of possibilities and sweat
started pouring out of me.
" Bugger it, we'll never find the right one in time." I
began to weep. After pulling all but one of twenty leavers
we stood there and looked at each other. " Well, you
better pray this does what it's supposed to do." he said
as he took a deep breath. We both placed our hand on
the leaver and began to pull.
" Look it's working, the wall is lifting."
I screamed with relief.
" Don't get so happy just yet, we gotta hope it gets high
enough in time for us to get under." Wade said looking
back at the cave in.

The tunnel ceiling above us began to crack and crumble,
dirt was blowing in all directions.
" Wade there must be something we can do to make the
bloody wall rise faster." The Professor then ran over to
the wall and tried lifting it.
" Wade, you'll never be able to lift it." I yelled as he
crawled under the wall.
" Well, I'm gonna try, I've got to do something." he said
as he positioned himself. As the wall moved higher my

eyes widened, I looked back up at the ceiling and back to the wall. I swallowed deep and ran to the wall to help him lift it.

" Wade, the wall should be high enough for us to get under!" I yelled.

" Quickly break off one of the leavers and wedge it under the wall for support." he yelled as he struggled to keep lifting. I ran over to the leavers and started to pull on them trying each one. " Wade! They won't break."

" Forget them, just get under the wall." I ran for the wall and slid on my side; I reached out for him and screamed. " Wade hurry!"

Then at that moment the tunnel collapsed, and with the force of the cave in I was thrown against the wall, everything went black. A short time later I was woken by the brightness of the sun. I slowly opened my eyes and placed my hand to the back of my head, realising what just happened I looked around for Wade.

" Wade!" I called out.

" How are you feeling? you took quite a hard knock." he said as he walked up behind me.

" Fine, I think. Just a bit of a headache, anyway, how did you get out?" I asked as he helped me to my feet.

" It was a bit tricky, but I managed to move in time."

" We better get moving we've got to find Brook and the crew." I said dusting myself off. Wade picket up his hat and we set out to find Brook. After some hours of hiking, we came across a small creek and decided to take a break before going any further. " Do you think we'll ever find Brook and the crew?" I asked. " Well, I don't think we'll find them today, but we'll keep looking till nightfall."

After refreshing ourselves we started to out again to continue our search for the others. Several hours on and still no sign of the crew and Brook and nightfall was getting close, so we came across an enormous hollow tree and decided to set up camp inside of it.
" Wade," I quietly said, " What do you think happened to the others?"
" We can only hope they're ok and looking for us." he paused and continued. " You mustn't give up hope, we'll find them you'll see." I snuggled in close to Wade to keep warm from the cool night air and drifted off to sleep.

With a jolt I was woken by a Macaw, one of the noisiest birds in existence, Wade then woke with a jump and hit his head on the side of the tree. I couldn't help myself; I just burst into laughter.
" Shh, quiet." Wade said.
" What is it? What's wrong?" my heart began to race.
" Someone's coming." I heard the sound approach I sat against the inside wall of the tree; a shadow crept around the entrance of the tree hollow; my eyes grew wider with the suspense and then a head popped around the corner and I screamed; it was Brook.
" G'day, where the bloody hell have you two been." He said as a smile came across his face.
" You wouldn't believe us if we told you." Wade said climbing out of the hollow.
" Did much of the equipment get damaged?" I asked.
" Nope, everything is intact." Brook answered.
" How about the food supplies?"
" Still got them." Brook replied.
" Great! I'm starving." I climbed out of the tree hollow and started looking for food.
" So, Wade, how long do you think till we locate the temple?" Brook asked as he wiped the sweat from his

forehead.
" Well, it's hard to tell. We still have to find the village,
and loosing so much time, Slade and Ali may be there by
now."
" We had better get moving then." I said standing up
with a mouthful of food.
" Yeah, we better move now. I don't think this weather
will hold out much longer, you know how unpredictable
rainforest weather is." Brook said as he looked towards
the sky.

Wade, Brook, the crew and I picked up the equipment
and supplies and once again began looking for the
village. Hiking through the dense greenery I had the
feeling we were being followed, I stopped walking and
surveyed the area around me. " What's wrong?" Wade
hollered back from halfway up the line.
" Wade! could you come down here, and hurry." I yelled
back as I continued to look around. Waiting for Wade I
looked harder into the jungle around me and then
noticed a dark figure moving in the shadows.   "
Wade, get your arse down here." I yelled out again.
" Hey, what's the problem." He said as he placed his
hand on my shoulder. I jumped with fright.
" Oh shit! Wade I think we are being followed." I said
looking up at him.
" Could you see who it is?" he asked as he looked
around. " No, but if we don't get moving, I'm sure we'll
find out who it is or who they are." We took one last look
and then joined the rest of the crew.
" What's going on?" Brook asked as he approached us.
" We think we are being followed." Wade explained.
" I don't think we are being followed, I know we are
being followed. I saw someone in the bushes." I said as I
stood back from Wade.

" Well, whoever it is we'll just have to keep watch. We must be getting close to the location of the village." said Brook.

We continued to search for the village, and the day crept on and still I could feel someone was following us. The afternoon began to creep in, and the air began to thicken, and clouds were building overhead.
" Guys, we better find some shelter soon or we'll be drenched."
" If I'm right, the village should be right behind that wall of trees." Brook pointed out as he walked up to us.
" Ah, Wade, why are the crew running away?" I questioned. Wade turned and looked behind us.
" I have no idea."
" Maybe I do." Brook said dropping his gear to the ground. Wade and I turned around and froze.
" See, I told you we were being followed." I too dropped my things on the ground.

" I don't believe it," Wade stood with his mouth open, " The Amazon tribe still exists."
" Well, you better believe it, we're surrounded by them." Brook said as he raised his hand in a non-aggressive manner. " It's true. The Amazon tribe is just women." my voice held a tone of wonder to it. Three of the tribe's warriors tied our hands behind our backs and lead us away, the rest of the tribe collected our things and followed on.

" Wade what do you think they will do with us?" I asked.
" We won't know until we get there." Rain began to fall, and the warrior women dragged us through the muddy paths into the village. It was a magnificent sight, all the huts were intact, it was like stepping back in time.

Ornate decorations adorned the doorways; it may just be a place time hasn't touched but there was a sense or order. We were taken to a large hut which looked to be the main one and above the door was a symbol. " Wade, did you see that?" I whispered.
" See what?"
" The symbol, above the entrance. It's a symbol of the sphere." I pointed out.
" Then that means this is the village of the Priestesses." Brook said looking around.

At that moment a highly decorated woman stepped into the light of the fire pit, following her was Slade and Ali.
" They'd have to have something to do with this." I said as my anger grew.
" So, you have finally made it this far." Slade said. " I was sure those traps would have taken care of you."
" FUCK YOU!" I spat the words out.
" Calm down." Wade said. " Talking like that won't do us any good."
" You're right Professor Wade; I could easily put you all to death." Slade began to smile at the thought.
" How could you. How could you do this to us." Brook questioned.
" It was quite easy," Ali said, " We needed the money."
" Take them away." Slade ordered.
" What do you plan to do with us." I questioned.
" I think I'll leave that to the Queen and her warriors." he said as they took us away.

Night fell, and we were thrown into a pit, they then covered it with branches and leaves. Cold and unsure of what would become of us, I snuggled close to wade and Brook and drifted off to sleep.

Chapter 5

The morning sunlight pushed its way through the coverings of the pit, and we could hear tribal members and Alia above, someone started moving the cover and as my eyes finished adjusting to the light I could see a figure, it was Ali." Ali, you arsehole!" I yelled at him." Shh, quiet." he whispered," I'm going to try get you out of
here."   "
Why should we trust you?" Wade questioned as he stood." How do we know it's not another trick; you've betrayed us already?" Brooks voice held anger as he points up at Ali." look, I don't have much time now. I'll be back." Ali said as he looked around. He then covered the pit over and left.

Days had passed since Ali spoke to us, I felt like giving up and I missed the sun. It was night fall, and the air was cool, then suddenly the pit cover was removed. Wade, Brook and I jumped to our feet and looked up to see who was there, it was the Queen, and he guards, I held tightly onto Wade's hand. The warriors threw down rope like vines for us to climb. Wade handed me the vines first and gave me a boost using his hands so began to climb up, when I reached the top two of the warriors helped me out and I was followed by Brook and Wade.

When we were all out of the pit the Queen ordered the warriors to tie our hands, Wade first then Brook. One of the women approached me and stood there and smiled, with my anger I called her a bitch and then flattened her with a right hook. She then hit the ground and looked up at me in disgust, she stood up and slapped me and tied my hands. We were lined up and torches were placed around Brook and Wade; I was pulled to the side. The Queen approached both men and began to inspect them as if they were for sale. She started with Brook; she walked around him for a short time and then stopped in front of him and looked closer to his face and then forced his mouth open I guess to look at his teeth. Satisfied with them she tore off his shirt and started to handle his body as if to see if it were ripe. She then moved to Wade, and repeated the inspection, when she had finished, she looked to the side at two of her warriors and gave a slight nod. Brook was taken away to one hut and Wade to another, and I was thrown into the pit.

Two days had passed since I was separated from the others and I was beginning to worry. I sat down and leaned against the wall of the pit waiting to see what was install. I could hear people coming towards the pit I stood up and went to a corner. The cover was thrown off, I looked up to see and then Brook and Wade were pushed back into the pit, I looked back up to the opening and the Queen looked over the edge and threw down some food, the pit was then recovered.

I ran over to the two men and helped them to their feet, their shirts were missing but the still had the rest of their clothes, the pit was once again uncovered, and skins were thrown in. I picked them up and placed them around the men's shoulders. " Are you ok? What did they do to you?" my voice was trembling from the cold of the pit. " They used us for their needs." Brook looked away as he spoke. " First they bathed us till our skin was raw, and then one at a time served us to the Queen, Brook first then me." Wade explained as he looked to the ground. " We were then separated and shared among the head warriors." said Brook as he looked about in a daze. I sat there between both men, Wade with his head on my shoulder and Brook with his head on my lap.

I think it was nightfall, it was getting hard to tell, everything was quiet not a sound could be heard and then a whisper filled the air in the pit. " It's me, Ali." The cover lifted. " Ok, now's the time." Ali said as he leaned over the edge of the pit, " Everyone's sleeping." He then tossed over three vines, Wade, Brook and I climbed out. Ali threw in the vines and covered the pit. " Here, you might want to put these on, I hope they fit, I took them from Slade." and he handed Wade and Brook each a shirt. " Ok, I'll take you out as far as I can out of the village." Ali whispered, " The temple is this way the path is behind the main hut." " Why are you helping us?" I asked confused. " Slade said there would be no killing, and the Queen was going to sacrifice you all." So, we continued to follow the path, the night grew dark and the jungle thicker.

We walked for at least an hour and still felt we couldn't trust Ali, but for our lives we had to. " Well, this is as far as I can go. Just follow the track and it will take you to the temple." Ali instructed us. " Wade, I still get the feeling we are being set up, something just isn't right." I whispered as I got closer to him.

" I don't trust the little shit either." Brook added. After walking for another couple of hours, we stopped to catch our breath before going any further. Wade stood up to stretch and at that moment the jungle fell silent.

" Wade, listen." I quietly spoke.

" What's wrong?"

" Don't you hear it? The drumming, it's coming from the village, they know we're gone." Brook's voice had a slight tremble as he spoke. " Come on, there's no time to lose." Wade said. He then grabbed my hand and we started running, the drums seemed as though they were getting louder. Looking behind me as we ran up the side of a hill, I could see the flaming torches trailing through the jungle. " Wade, they're coming!" I yelled. " Let's hope the temple is close." Brook yelled as he turned back to us. I looked back again to see, and they were gaining on us, I tripped on vines and fell. " WADE!" I screamed.

Wade stopped and ran back to help me to me feet, we looked back and could see the warriors were getting closer. " Come on, this way." Brook called to us as he ran to the right of the track. Wade took my hand and we followed Brook through the thick bushes, tearing my shirt as I ran through. With the sounds of the tribe behind us we crouched behind a thick veil of vines. " Wade, in case we don't come out of this alive," I said then Brook interrupted. " Quiet, they're coming." I looked to wade and whispered. " I love you." He then looked back to me and smiled, at that moment the tribe started running past. So, we couldn't be seen, we crouched as low as we could behind the vines.

" Ok, I think they're gone." Brook said as he looked through the vines. As we began to stand, we could hear someone coming behind us. Brook turned around and said, " Ah guys, I think we've been found." As I stood up, I carefully picked up a piece of branch that was lying on the ground next to me and spunk around with all my strength and hit the person as hard as I possibly could, the person's body hit the ground. Wade knelt to check it and said, " She's out cold, but still alive." " Damn!" I grumbled, " I broke a nail." I dropped the chunk of wood. I looked at Brook and Wade, and they were just staring at me. " Well, what are we waiting for, let's get going." I casually said as I walked past them.

The tribe was gone, and we kept on looking for the temple. It was now early hours of the morning but still quite dark, and as we walked through the jungle, we noticed a peacefulness. " Wade, look." I ran ahead. " What is it?" " It looks like some kind of marker." Brook explained. " A marker for what exactly?" Wade questioned. I pulled off the vines that covered the post to see it clearly. " Oh my god. I don't believe it; it's a marker for the temple." I said as I brushed my hair from my face. " At least we are going in the right direction." Wade's voice had a sound of relief to it. We sat there to rest until sunrise before going any further as it was only a couple of hours away. " When I get home, I'm going to soak in a steaming hot bath, and after that, I'll take another one." I said placing my hands behind my head. " Sounds good. I might take one too." Wade looked at me from the corner of his eye. " Oh please, save it for later you guys, you're making me sick." Brook said as he places his hands around his neck.

The sky began to get lighter, and the air warmer and the Macaw started its loud obnoxious call. " Ok, let's get moving." Brook instructed. " We better, you never know when the Amazons will pop up." Wade said as he helped me to my feet. " Well, it looks like we should head in that direction according to the marker." I stood taking one last look and pointing in the direction. We started up the overgrown trail in search of the temple, the day went on and no more markers were seen. " Maybe we went in the wrong direction." I stopped to catch my breath. " Maybe not." Wade said. " What?" I straightened up. " Look, over there." Wade was pointing to a broken-down tree. Brook ran over to the tree and started scraping off the moss. " You're right, it's another marker." Brook continued pulling off the moss, " We must be getting closer, this one's etched in gold."
" Come on, this way." Wade took my hand to help me keep moving. We changed direction to follow the marker, the path was even harder to follow than the last, but we pushed on. " Guys look, it's another." I pointed out a stone pillar.
" Looks like this one takes us to that mountain." Wade was translating the markings.
" You don't think the temple could be the mountain, do you?" I questioned. " Could be, it could even be in the mountain." Brook replied as he looked on.

We continued through the jungle towards the mountain that lay ahead hoping our journey would soon be over. Midday has past, and the heat was intense, and the air was thick afternoon shadows were being cast, the trail seemed endless, but we kept moving on. The overgrown trail started to thin out, and it was much easier to see. " Guys look, the trail, it's paved." I said as I leaned down to touch it. " You're right, we must be almost there."

Wade to touching the path. " Don't you think it's a little strange that we've had no trouble with the Amazons." Brook surveyed our surroundings. " Come to think of it, it is." I replied as I stood up and looked around. " Well, whatever they are up to, we had better be careful and stay alert." Wade had a cautious tone to his voice. " Right, let's get moving, we don't want to be out in the open when night falls." Brook suggested.

We followed the stone path and still no sign of anyone. The sun had now set, and the moon was full and the moonlight through the jungle canopy lit up the path. Most of the plants on either side of the path faced away so it was much easier to follow and in the brightness of the moonlight something caught my eye. " Wade, look, a statue." Brook approached it and cleared of the vines, " It looks to be a statue of a High Priestess."
" I guess they believe the statue will guard the temple." Wade too approached the statue. I looked at the statue for a moment and then turned, stunned at its overpowering appearance I was unable to speak, all I could do was stare.

" Wow shit!" Brook said with amazement. " I don't believe it; we finally found it." Wade stepped back from the stature. " The temple." I said with a gasp. The temple was enormous, it wasn't just in the mountain, it was the mountain. The entrance was overgrown in vines, but you could see the design in the moonlight. Above the entrance was gold statue of the sphere, the door is a gold archway, and both sides were stone pillars, a little decayed but still standing. On entering the walls were heavily cracked and had partly crumbled away, but still a magnificent sight to behold.

" Come on, let's go in." Brook led the way as he took the first step inside. Wade and I followed on; we entered the first room looking around us as we went. The room was filled with stone statues, the walls were trimmed with gold figurines, so we separated to look at everything in the room. " Try not to touch anything, it may be rigged up to something." I warned both men. " Hey guys, come over here, look what I've found." Brook called out from the other side of the room, " It's the staff and headpiece of the High Priestess." Brook held them up for us to see. " And they've recently been used." Wade said as he took a closer look. Full of curiosity, I left that room anxious to see what was in the next. The interior of this room was in better condition than the last. The floor had gold melted into it making spectacular patterns and the ceiling had gold images scattered in all directions, and at the end of the hall were two giant timber doors.

" Wade!" I called out, " Come look at this." " Wow! I've never seen so much gold." Wade said as he walked up behind me. " This is incredible, the architecture is so amazing." Brook's voice echoed. " Do you think the sphere is behind those doors?" I asked Wade. " Maybe, but there's only one way to find out." Wade said as he took a step closer to the doors. " Wait a minute, there's something wrong." Brook stood in front of us.   " What's wrong? There's nobody here." I looked around us. " That's what I mean, there's something not right here." Brook was sounding worried. " He's right you know. They know we are coming so you think they'd be guarding the joint, this could very well be a trap." Wade then turned around surveying the room where we stood. " Come on, I'm still going through these doors, with or without you." I turned and walked up to the doors. " Wait!" both men yelled, " We're coming!"

Walking through the great hall, I began to get an eerie feeling of being watched. " Do you feel it?" I asked Wade. " There's definitely something." All three of us stood at the massive doors, still unsure of what was on the other side. We turned to look behind us to see if anyone was there, but there was no one.
" How strange."
" What's that." Brook looked back at me.
" Those statues."
" What about them." Wade asked looking back at them.
" I'm pretty sure they weren't there before." I said feeling very puzzled.
" It's not like they can get up and walk now is it." Brook turned back to the doors.

All three of us placed our hands on the giant doors and started to push them open, and with the weight of the doors they were moving very slowly. " How on earth did they ever get these doors here in the first place, what did they do? enslave a few dozen men?" Brook mumbled as he pushes the doors. " In actual fact yes, they enslave twenty or so men in total." I replied. " The Amazon women sacrificed them as they didn't need them anymore." answered Wade.

As the doors finally opened, the brightest purest light shone around us with a blinding effect, we placed our hands above our eyes to shield them. After a few moments the light dimmed so we were then able to see.
" Oh, my hell." I said as my mouth dropped open.
" Bloody hell." Brook said as he gazed at the walls.
" My god." Wade looked up at the ceiling. The room was in immaculate condition, the walls were in the whitest of white, the ceiling went into the shape of a dome, great white balconies finished in gold came out of the walls

and in the centre of the room was a gold cage standing tall, with a pillar of light descending from crystal lenses in the highest point of the ceiling. " Brook, Wade, remember, no man can touch the sphere, so the legend goes only a woman can touch it." I warned.

We walked further into the room still taken by its beauty. I slowly approached the raised platform the golden cage stood upon. Feeling the warmth and the energy of the sphere I began to walk up the steps leading to it. " Don't take another step!" a voice echoed around the room. I stepped back from the platform and looked in all directions to see where the voice was coming from. " Who is it? Show yourself!" I demanded. " Have you forgotten me already."
" Slade! enough of your stupid games, show yourself." I yelled with more anger. " Look! In the upper balcony." Wade pointed out as he walked over to me. " How did you know we were going to be here?" Brook bellowed from the other side of the room. " Surely you can't be completely stupid, my faithful assistant Ali told me everything." Slade began to laugh.
" You son of a bitch Slade!" I yelled at him as I walked closer to the balcony. " Flattery will get you nowhere my dear."

We were quickly surrounded by the tribe from all directions, the Queen appeared by Slade and so did Ali with a few of the warriors. The cage was lifted from the sphere and Brook, Wade and I were taken onto the platform and held by the sphere.
" What are you going to do with us?" I yelled to Slade.
" I'm going to get one of you to touch the sphere." Slade then sent Ali down. " You bastard!" Brook yelled. Ali stepped onto the platform and took my wrist. " Come

along deary, you can have the honour of going first." Ali
started dragging me closer to the sphere. " No!" I
screamed as I struggled to get away. " Let her go you
mongrel." Wade yelled trying to free himself. Brook then
kicked out his foot tripping Ali, as he fell, I was able to
break loose causing Ali to fall against the sphere.

" Ali! No!" Slade yelled out leaning over the balconies
edge. Ali began to scream in pain, " Slade! Help me!" A
red mist began to appear circling his body, sweat poured
from his head and bloody ran from his ears. Flashes of
light lit up his body then a thundering like sound echoed
throughout the room and with the final screams of help
Ali vanished, never to be seen again. The room was quiet
once more, and the only sound to be heard was the
heavy breathing of the tribe surrounding us.

" You bitch!" Slade screamed as he pulled out a gun. "
Slade No!" I screamed looking up at him. At that
moment Slade fired the gun, I dived onto the floor,
missing me the bullet hits the warrior behind me, and
she fell to the floor, dead. Brook and Wade knocked the
warriors holding them out of the way. Slade then fired
the gun again missing us and hitting the wall. The bullet
then ricochets from wall to wall, people were running in
all directions, Wade, Brook and I ran under the balcony.
A spear was thrown from the balcony and landed in
front of us." Stay here, I'll be right back." Wade said.

Wade ran out and picked up the spear and aimed it at
Slade. Seeing one of the warriors about to throw a spear
at Wade, Brook ran out and tackled him, and at that
moment the bullet stopped. " Wade!" I screamed
running out to them.
" What happened to the bullet?" Wade asked. " It hit the

warrior."
" No need to worry," Slade announced, " I have more."
Slade then held up the gun and started to laugh. Full of
anger I picked up the spear and threw it with everything
I had. The spear whistled through the air as is it flew just
missing Slade and piercing the wall beside him. " Shit!" I
yelled as I placed my hands to the sides of my face. "
Good try, but not good enough." Slade said as he pointed
the gun in my direction. As Slade pulled the trigger, the
Queen plunged a dagger into his back the gun fired but
missed.

Slade fell from the balcony and landed on the stone floor
in front of me, blood ran from knife wound and from the
crack in his head. " Wade, where did the bullet go?" I
yelled.
" I didn't see."
" The sphere, it's cracking!" Brook yelled as he came to
his feet, " The bullet must have hit the sphere." The walls
and ceiling began to crack and crumble. The Queen and
her guards started to panic, the sides of the balcony
started to crumble beneath them. The floor around the
sphere opened and flames blew up towards the ceiling, I
turned and started running for the doors, but the flames
roared up in front of me. Giant pieces of golden beams
fell around me; I turned to look for Wade but could not
see him. I looked up to the Queen and her guards, it
looked as though they were aging right before my eyes I
had never seen anything like it, they went from young
virile women to frail bodied old ladies and as the temple
shook they lost their footing and fell into the pit of fire
followed by the balcony where they once stood.

" WADE!" I screamed. " Over here." He yelled back.
" I can't see you!" " Don't move I'll come for you." Tribes'

women were running in all directions screaming as they went, large chunks of stone fell away from the walls crashing to the floor shattering the marble. " Wade! where the hell are you." I called out but there was no answer. I closed my eyes and held my breath as I ran and jumped into the air, hitting the ground on the other side I steadied myself to look for Brook and Wade. " Wade, Brook!" I screamed, " Where are you guys." Dirt and rocks started caving in where the balcony once was and through large cracks and holes in the walls. " WADE!" I screamed out once again. " I'm here." he yelled. I turned and could just see him standing near the huge doors at the entrance to the room. " Look Out!" Brook yelled. I turned to his direction and as I did a large pillar was beginning to crumble and fall in my direction, I screamed. Brook ran and dived, pushing me out of its path.

I landed just to the side of where I was standing, the pillar came crashing down on Brook covering him in debris. " Brook!" I screamed as I reached out to him. At that moment a silence filled the remains of the temple room, and all that could be heard was the crackling of the fire and the odd stone that fell. With tears in my eyes I lifted my head and looked around. " Wade." I paused, " Wade." " Over here." he answered. I stood up to see where he was standing, from the brightness of the flames I placed my hand in front of my eyes to shield them from the heat. I walked through the rubble towards Wade, I could see he was holding something. " Wade, what is it?" I yelled from the other side of the room. " It's a fragment of the sphere. I thought we better take something back to prove we found The Sphere of Eternal Life." he answered. " Wade." " Sh. Quiet." he said cutting me off. " What's wrong?" I stood still.

As sudden as it stopped the ground began to shake, even harder than before. I turned and ran for the door, the walls were falling from all directions, I looked up through the dust and could see Wade standing at the doors. " Come on, hurry, you can do it." Wade yelled stepping forward. I pushed myself harder, and in doing so I tripped and fell. " Ah shit." I mumbled as I hit the ground. Filled with pain I slowly rose to my feet. " Watch out!" Wade yelled. I looked up and a large portion of the ceiling had broken away and was falling above me. I dived out of its path and landed beside a broken statue, the stone ceiling shattered as it hit the floor showering the room with fragments.

Wade looked out through the doors and back again. " Come on!" he yelled, " The entire mountain could come down any minute." " I'm coming as fast as I can!" As I took a step the ground opened beneath me, I looked over to Wade and screamed, " Wade, help me!" Wade dropped the fragment of the sphere and came running, and as I fell, he leaped for my hands and grabbing them as my arms went past. With flames shooting up behind me I screamed, " Wade, hurry." I finally got a foothold, so I push with my feet, Wade dragged me up out of the hole and pulled me to safety. " You, ok?" he asked. " I'll be much better once we get the hell out of here." Wade took my hand and we ran out of the room.

We entered the great hall, pillars were falling like a domino effect, statues toppled over crashing to the floor. " Wade. Which way?" " This way, down here." We ran to the right of the hall with stone and earth falling behind us. " Come on, there's not much further now." Wade yelled. The roar of the falling mountain was almost deafening, with the impact of earth, stone, gold and

marble hearing was close to impossible. We continued running dodging rocks as we went, as we were a few feet from the final room, the floor opened and flames exploded into the air in front of us. " What are we going to do now?" I asked. " I don't know, let me think." " Do you think you could think a little faster! "I sarcastically yelled. " Ok, I think I've got something, wait here, I'll be right back."
"Wade! come on." He then threw a couple of vines over a stone beam and twisted them together.

" Ok. you go first, just hold on tight." He instructed. " If I don't make this, I'm coming back to kill you." I said as I took hold of the vines. " Well, what the hell are you waiting for." He yelled. I then stepped back and began to run, leaping off the edge I screamed as I flew through the air. " Now let go!" Wade yelled out from the other side of the fire. " Are you sure?" I asked. " Yes, damn it!" I let go of the vines and let out a screech and hit the ground with a roll.
" Ok, I'm coming across now, stand back."
" Wade hurry, the beam is starting to break." Wade then took run up grabbing hole of the vines as he left the ground. " Oh Shit!" he yelled as he flew over the flames. " WADE!" I screamed as I watched the beam break and crumble to nothing. I closed my eyes and turned away from in fear that he had fallen into the fire.

" Well, you can't just sit there forever if you wish to get out of here alive." a voice came out of the dust. Looking up I turned to see where the voice came from, it was Wade, I jumped to my feet and kissed him. " I thought you had fallen into the fire." I said holding his face. " I really don't think now's the time for this." We started running for the entrance, the statues that were placed

around the walls were crumbling, huge boulders fell
from the ceiling exploding as the hit the ground. " Wade,
the stairs are gone." " We'll have to jump for it." he said
looking on. A backdraft had filled the hall and the rush
of air was hot, I turned to look and shouted, " Wade,
we'll have to hurry there's a huge arse fireball coming for
us." We stepped back and started running. " We aren't
going to make it!" I yelled. " Will you shut up and bloody
run." he ordered. With the explosion and force of the
fireball we were picked up and thrown out of the temple
entrance and into a nearby thicket. The ground
surrounding the mountain shook fiercely and as we
looked up to see the temple the top of the mountain
exploded showering the surrounding jungle in debris.
The sides of the mountain blew out causing the rest of it
to crumble and sink beneath the earth. Molten lava
came to the surface hardening as it cooled, sealing where
the mountain, temple, once stood.

In a matter of minutes, it had all ended and the jungle
was peaceful once more. " Wade?" " Yes." " They'll never
believe us you know." I said looking towards the temple
site. " Maybe it just wasn't meant to happen." he
answered as he stood up from the bush. " Maybe, maybe
not." I said walking in front of him. " Wait a minute." he
said. " What's wrong?" I asked confused. " Over there, by
that tree." Wade started walking away. " It looks like
part of a crystal." I followed him. " I don't believe it." he
said turning to me. " It looks like we can prove the
temple did exist after all." I said as I approached. " Yeah,
and that there was a sphere, The Sphere of Eternal Life."
he said.

We started our way through the jungle, back through the
towns to make our way back to Sydney and back to the

university where the fragment will be prepared for the
museum for the people to see and to ignite the
imaginations of those to come.

THE END.

Book 3

Dark Hunger

Chapter 1

Once again night has thrown its dark blanket over the city and my hungry passion needed to be satisfied and I knew just the place to feed this hunger. For the tasty sensual delights that flock to this Human Marketplace, where one is guaranteed to meet a fine specimen that can be easily detained for one's pleasure and entertainment, and for me it's virgin territory and ripe for the picking.

The air was thick and heavy with the heat of bodies that danced wildly to the rhythmic persuasion of the music. I made my way through the crowd like a thief in the night, stealing glances from those who lay in my path. I stood still for a moment taking note who would be my new target, my victim, for this feast full night. I began to weave my way through the dance floor when I noticed him watching, watching my every move.

He was tall, solid, muscular build with dark hair and blue eyes. From his look and his energy, he would be the one I would claim. I made my place in the centre of the floor and began to cast my spell. Moving my body to the seductive smoothness of the music, I worked my hypnotic power of persuasion around my beautiful victim. Like a moth to a flame, I lured him closer to my web where he would never escape. The intensity of the music grew filling the room with more excitement and passion, my lustful grip magnified as the stranger approached. Closer he came, with the short space between us, the air began to burn with steam rising from our bodies. With the final twist of my enchantment, I flooded his eyes with mine and filled him with pure erotic desire. He reached out to me gripping me around my waist pulling me close, into his heavily chiselled body, he was trapped, mine to play with, to feast upon with my desires.

As we danced, he started to kiss me, and I could feel his soul cry for release. his manhood grew and hardened to its full potential as he pressed against my body; his fiery passion growing stronger. Little did he know what was to become of him, soon enough he would learn of his fate, but he will be helpless.

His tongue was hot and moist as it left my lips. I could hear his heartbeat and his blood rush through his veins as he began to kiss and lick my neck. I drew back from him raised an eyebrow and then slowly danced around him like a snake about to strike its prey. Deeper he fell into my bottomless pit. I could feel the pain and ecstasy screaming and begging to be released. I came in close to him once again feeling his hands slide over my arse rubbing me against his firm erect manhood; with his shirt open I could see his moistened chest heave with pleasure and the veins in his neck began to show and beat with a passionate rhythm. Time grew near for his misery to end and ending it would be my pleasure. I licked and bit at his nipples letting both of us succumb to the mysteries of the night. He moaned and threw his head back as I continued to pleasure is body, and then the time was right, his body was ready. I gazed into his eyes and made my way to the exit. Like a lost dog he followed, helpless and unaware of his fate.

As a mindless zombie he followed as we walked for a short time to a darkened ally. I stepped into the shadows and whispered to him to come with me; he then stepped into the endless shadow. Pulling him closer to me we kissed; I could feel his hot moist tongue pass my lips. The primal medieval fire began to rage in me like it did centuries before. The forces of night flowed through and around me, the sounds of his soul screeched its deafening tones begging for release. In an instant my handsome stranger fell to the ground, lifeless like a rag doll, the taste of his soul was powerful but sweet, my hunger was satisfied. I emerged from the blackness of the shadow to retreat, and to rest, ready to haunt my new domain.

Looking out into the birth of a fresh new night, I could feel arousing sounds of souls calling to me, daring me to play with them. I have grown accustomed to the black disease that flowed through my veins, and I could feel it's carnal urge to delight my craving. The dark heart of midnight approached and the mindless nightlife of the mortals that wondered this earthly plain, awaited my arrival so that they may entertain me with their feeble efforts of seduction. Dressed in black plastic attire and full-length coat, I ventured forth with my next plan of attack in place.

The night air was cool, laced with fine droplets of moisture form the dew that was beginning to settle in, and the streets reflected light from the full moon the drifted in the murky sea of night. As I approached the crowded city streets where I will soon twist and subdue the mind of my next pathetic male mortal.

A sound caught my attention; I could feel the presence of another that lives in the isolation where I reside. I stopped to study my surroundings, to seek this intruder, as this place I roam was mine to rule and feed upon, and I had no mind to share my kills. In a moment's breath the air stopped and went silent and only the sound of footsteps could be heard, approaching me from behind. I turned to see who was the fool that dare trespass on my grounds and expected to live, then swift like the wind flew past and stood before me. I summoned the dark force that lay within me to reveal itself and the turned to face the fool that dare challenge me. Our eyes met, and we began to size each other up. He was good looking, medium build close to my height and looked about one hundred and fifty and should have enough sense not to take on another of his kind who is two hundred years his elder, as the older one is, the more power and strength one gathers; but still the child wanted to take me on even if it meant his death.

The young kin leapt into the air with a choir of screams surrounding him; his black cape flowing in the wall of solid air he summoned. I turned and through myself from the path of the oncoming assault. The solid air hit the ground with a loud thunderous clap, cracking the pathway where I stood. I rose from the ground and the elevated myself some feet above the street willing a bench from its place of rest hurling it at my kin, knocking him out of the sky. I propelled myself to where he fell and knelt beside the disabled body and waited for his eyes to open. A deep breath entered his body and his eyes opened and looked up at me, he smiled so I smiled back and then thrusted my clawed hand into his chest and tore his heart from its cavity. I then stood and watch as his remains turn into dust and drift off into the wind.

Feeling weary from the brief but strenuous battle I desperately needed a kill to regain my strength. I retreated into the shadow of a nearby building when hearing the footsteps of an approaching human. From the scent of the mortal, I could tell it was male; in his mid-twenties medium build and as far as I was concerned, he was perfect. Silently I waited, his scent growing stronger, then hearing the enticing beat of his heart I stepped out of the shadow and stopped the victim with a smile for I could tell what his body desired.

As he leaned forward to touch and kiss me, I took hold of him by the throat and feasted on the splendid mortal, feeling his erotic energy and blood fill my veins. This one was indeed my sweetest kill yet, shame I needed a fix so soon there was so much more I could have done with this human boy, but when one is in need of nourishment one must satisfy the craving.

The night was quickly passing as there was not much time left to enjoy the pleasure that walk the streets. So, with the short time that was left for me I walked amongst the fanciful delights and just admired the excellent male bodies of the human race and the sweet aroma that each one had to offer. After surveying the potential game, I returned to me haven to rest and lay in wait for my next night of pleasure.

Chapter 2

Time began passing, I've been in this droll city for some months now and usually I have moved on by this time, but the mortals here amuse me. After centuries of wondering this morbid earth in darkness I should have grown accustomed to the loneliness that comes with it but unfortunately one does not, yes, we can live forever, but we still have other needs, and these needs are beginning to grow fiercely inside of me. The is calling and my hunger grows with every minute.

The dark shield of night is blacker than usual with no moon or stars to hold me back; this makes it more exciting for play. I leapt from the balcony of my abode and glided to the streets of my playground to begin my hunt. As I landed, I heard the shuffled of feet and a gasp of air, in a second, I turned and smiled, and in the next half a second, I snapped the mortals' neck, she fell like a sack on manure. I then turned and made my way to where mortals feel free to give away their souls for any price no matter what they must pay. The alluring music of souls and rhythmic beating blood grew louder as I entered the populated streets of nightlife.

Dressed in every kind of attire young male street walkers followed my every step with eyes that reflected the dull lights hoping that I would prey upon them for their services, no chance for what they offer is tainted.

With an impact my attention was caught by an aroma, a rather intriguing one. I followed it into the centre of the Human Marketplace where a new venue has opened. I for a moment feeling the exciting new scent tease me, the doorman invited me to enter this banquet hall. Entering the club, the alluring scent wrapped me up and drew me closer. I was finding it hard to control my primal urge as it was begging to be released, I turned from the crowd to gain control of my dark desire do I may continue my hunt. I felt hand touch my shoulder and a smooth sounding young male voice enquired to my health, a hot shiver electrified my body the scent was powerful, it was he. I turned to see his face he was indeed beautiful. This was very strange, I felt trapped, bewitched, the blackness in me had settled yet still violent. This young specimen took me by the hand and lead me to where he sat, this young morsel seemed familiar somehow, his soul I had crossed once before, as to when I couldn't be sure. He signalled to a bartender, and a drink of red liquid was placed in a glass and presented to me. I placed the glass beneath my nose and breathed in the aroma, it didn't smell like human or animal, the young man leaned over and whispered to my ear explaining it was a Bloody Mary and that his name was Trey, he sat back in his chair and smiled.

The club was perfectly lit mostly in darkness; I looked over to where people were dancing there were a handful of lights but still dark enough for pleasure. The music was hypnotic everyone danced like mindless puppets trying to seduce any pitiful onlooker. Trey touched my hand and made a motion for the dance floor I accepted the offer and we drifted to the area. The music changed, and it was time to get serious; the primal urges began rising inside of me manifesting themselves throughout the club taking control of the night, manipulating the minds and bodies of those it touched.

Trey began to unbutton the red plastic shirt I wore and run his fingers over my chest. As the black evil in me started to boil I could smell the sweetness in his blood as it rose with the steam of his body heat. This human was special; he awoke desires in me I had not felt in centuries. His young tender lips touched mine and I could feel the blood that filled them, to taste him would make it complete but I could not feed upon this one for I had plans for him.

We left the club after the end of the song and made our way to Trey's' place of residence. He opened the door of the apartment and entered; I could only stand there and wait to be invited to enter as that was the only way I could pass through the door. Trey then looked at me and said " You can come in " I could feel the barrier lift as he spoke these words, he closed the door behind me and removed my coat. I don't like to waste time when it comes to these matters, this time must be quick for I have not yet fed, and I grow weaker as the night goes on. Trey led me to his bed and began to undress me. He's a beautiful looking boy in his early twenties, medium build almost six feet with brown/blonde hair and green eyes.

After removing our shirts, he began to kiss my neck working his way down my chest then rolling his tongue around and across my nipples, dizziness filled my head as I fought the evil that wanted to take over and rule this moment. I took him by the chin and placed his lips to mine. The heat within his lips began to burn, the taste of his moist warm tongue was sweet like candy. I could feel the rush of blood beneath his soft skin the pain of this pleasure was unlike any sunrise.

With forces raging I threw Trey onto the bed, he seemed to like this, he sat upright placing his hands on my belt buckle and proceeded to undo my belt and then my black leather jeans; then looking up at me gave me a smile and began with sexual pleasures I had not encountered before. Sweat fell from my brow as he suckled my aroused manhood, the heat of his mouth and wetness of his tongue as it rubbed my hardness shattered the evil anger that burned in my blood. As Trey continued to remove my jeans and began to unbutton his own and then laying back onto the bed, I looked down to him then bent over and slowly peeling off the blue fitted jeans he wore. I dropped them to the floor and like a snake glided up his body sliding my tongue as I went, his body arched tensing muscles on his legs and back. He moaned griping my hair and pulling my lips to his. The heat of our bodies grew like the flames of hell burning in my black heart. He rolled over then raising himself to his knees, I knelt behind him wrapping my arms around him gently biting at his neck trying not to tear the veins out that pump under his skin. Moving his arse in circular motion against my erect firmness he began begging me to take him. Everything was wet from sweat, the bed clothes, our bodies, the air, in that moment I thrusted my pulsating shaft into his body, Trey's head jerked back with a loud moan full sigh of the pleasurable pain he felt as he pushed and pulled himself back and forth. The lust and ecstasy stormed its way through my body as I felt the tense tightening of muscles inside of Trey's body.

I began to reach point of explosion and the blackness inside of me began to tear at my skin, He yelled for me to push harder, I could feel the change in me taking place. The pictures on the wall shook, the windows began to crack, our bodies moved faster. Trey and I reached climax and felt the release within, the pictures and the windows shattered exploding as we screamed with erotic animalistic pleasure. We both fell to the bed exhausted; I was weak and needed to feed, I dressed quickly and left before he could regain consciousness and ask any questions.

There were only a few short hours of darkness left I desperately needed to feed, I went back to where the street walkers were as it were easier to take one of them than to find a clean human. As before their eyes danced as I walked by them, a walker came from the shadow of a building and approached me with sexual favours, I accepted and took him to a lightless park nearby. He wasn't the greatest looking creature, but he would do. We stopped under a bridge as it was all he deserved; I then let the ancient black evil in me take over. I turned seizing him by the neck with my clawed hand, his blood flowed freely as I tore out his jugular. He began to scream, to keep him silent I pierced his throat with a claw, a short time later I snapped his neck and left him where he lay. His blood and strength flowed me as tainted as it was it had to do; sunrise was closer. I ran through the streets to my abode, sunrise just minutes away I leapt onto the wall of my building climbing my way to my balcony, I hurled myself over the top and closed the timber doors behind me just in time to stop the sun from killing my existence. I retired to my stone-cold tomb ready to prey upon this pathetic city of humans.

Chapter 3

From the impure feast I had the night had left a foul taste in my mouth and a feeling of weakness which means I must make a kill early this eve if I am to last the night. The sun has set; now the hunt will begin. I've stepped out onto the balcony to scan the killing field that lay before me. Someone young and fresh will do nicely, maybe eighteen or so there is usually a couple that hang around the park at this time. They're close, I can smell them. With no one in sight, I leapt off the balcony and landed in the ally beside my building, looking around I made my way to the park where my appetisers would be waiting.

As I walked further into the park the two boys came into sight. One of them approached me for a cigarette, I handed one to him then saying to him he seemed a little young to be wandering around, he just smiled and said thanks and turned to walk away, as he did I placed my hand on his shoulder and asked if I could buy him a drink, he didn't seem to mind the suggestion. He signalled to the other young guy he was with, and they went their separate ways. We set off toward the city hotels only to make a slight detour down a back road that led to nowhere but only to the bittersweet end to my young friend. Perfection I thought as I drank the last drop from his young but well-formed body. It was refreshing to have the taste of young untainted blood a stimulating energy boost something was hard to come by; I wiped the blood from the corners of my mouth and left the ally.

Being in two minds of how I should entertain myself, I turned and walked away from the city nightlife and wandered down to the shoreline on the river and inspect what activity would be on display. On my approach, music, laughter and excitement could be heard; it seems to be some kind of street party, amusing I thought as I got nearer this looked to be quite entertaining. There were mortals everywhere, all kinds of shapes and sizes, quite enticing, unfortunately it wasn't only for the male population of the human race, but one can't have everything. Like spider weaving a web I made my way through the crowd, the energy and smell of the male specimens that surrounded me was indeed evocative, I felt bewitched and found it hard to contain myself, if this was heaven; well, my heaven, I had found it.

" So where have you been."

I stopped moving and turned to see who spoke these words. I looked around, but I could not see the owner of this voice.

" Over Here."

It was Trey, he remembered me. Sometimes it's better to feast upon a mate then let them live even if they are different. I had broken my own cardinal rule, but his aroma caught my senses and I could not resist.

" What happened the other night, did I do something wrong?" Trey asked as he touched my face, the electricity in his skin was seductive. I simply told him I had some business to take care of.

" I do hope you stick around for a while, at least until it's finished, maybe we could have some more fun later. Oh, by the way this is Bobby, we've been friends for a number of years."

" I don't think that will be a problem." I replied as I admired Trey's little friend. Bobby was something one could not help but look at and admire. He was indeed a very fine specimen, with blonde hair, steel grey eyes enclosed with a deep blue ring of colour around the grey, his skin was moderately tanned and his body well-toned and best of all well-formed veins around his throat. Feeding on this one would be a treat.

Trey took me by the hand and lead me to where other humans were dancing in the street, at least back in my time one was asked to dance not just dragged out, but it was pleasing. As Trey and I was dancing Bobby was off to the side watching us, watching me, watching my every move. I could see and feel what he wanted, and it had nothing to do with dancing. Trey began to run his hands over my body then pressing himself against me, I could hear the beating of his heart grow louder as it beat in time with the music, I closed my eyes and lost myself with him but keeping Bobby in the back on my mind.

Trey's hand found its way to my crotch, the warmth of his hand was pleasing, opening my eyes Trey turned his back to me, motioning his body with the rhythm and slid down my body then back up, he placed the side of his head next to mine baring his naked neck. The satanic evil that lived in me began to boil and creep its way to the surface. This familiar feeling, I had encountered with Trey's soul had gripped my attention, I did not understand the feeling of meeting him before, for I could not think where. His face was not familiar, I hadn't seen him in any another country, unless, he was connected to someone in my pastas to whom I can't be sure.

Trey started to kiss my neck, with these thoughts in my head I held his face in my hands and said I had to leave and to meet me at the club the next night where we had first met. I kissed him and left. With these thoughts and memories spinning in my head I wandered through the streets back to me place of rest.

Some short blocks from my building I could hear footsteps approaching from behind, I leapt into the branches of a nearby tree to investigate the stupid mortal that would follow. I was Bobby, he stood beneath the tree for a moment. This indeed would make a good snack. So, I drifted from the tree to the ground behind him and asked if he was looking for me, he turned and smiled, so I smiled back then let the vile beast in me take control. Grabbing him by the throat I summoned solid masses of air beneath us and propelled both of us into the black heart of the night sky. The boy tried to struggle but it was useless, there was no place he could go except down. We were now above the buildings and what people that could be seen looked like ants. I looked to my handsome meal and flashed my needle point teeth, the painful horror took place in his eyes of what was to become of him; I ferociously kissed him tearing into his lower lip, blood flowed and filled my mouth; such a sweet nectar. He screamed in pain and at the same time choked on the blood that filled his throat. He tried to speak but couldn't, I could see the life in his eyes slip away; I licked the blood that dripped from his chin, then tore into his throat like a rabid dog and drank till almost the last drop then stopped to look at him, his eyes were barely open. He looked up to my eyes and spluttered through the blood " Please let me go." So, I told him his wish was my command, without another thought I let him go. He fell back to the street with an exploding sound and the noise of car alarms as he impacted a parked car. Feeling quite plethoric I descended to the car where he lay, his body all twisted and broken, eyes still open.

A crowd of footsteps came rushing from every direction, I scaled the building wall behind me in order not to be seen and climbed my way to the top to where I could watch. Women were screaming, and men were yelling for the police and an ambulance, in the distance the sirens could be heard. I grew board of watching and left. Leaping from building to building I reached mine where I sat on the balcony and started into the city lights that filled the night sky, trying to figure out the familiarity with Trey and hi soul. I searched every memory to find this mystery. My skin began to burn, I looked up, morning was approaching it was time to retreat.

Chapter 4

As I slept visions of the past played in my head like the
repeats of an old movie. My memory searched the many
places I had ventured, the many places I had preyed
upon, and still I could not find any relation to the feeling
I had about Trey. For some reason my mind came to rest
on a place that appeared to be a riverside town. Heavy
with fog, and it seemed to be in the year eighteen twenty
give or take a year, and for a town of its size it certainly
had a very good choosing of men and traders from
further north. The docks were always alive with new and
exciting things to play with and feed upon, such as
paddle steamers that brought rich gamblers aboard the
floating casinos and the gambling houses in the centre of
town. Men and women dressed in the finest of fabrics
adorned in precious trinkets and alluring scents.

My mind went deeper into this memory, and I began to
feel a sense of familiarity maybe this was the place of
Treys recognition. I walked along the docks winding in
and out of the crowds of people that conducted their
business, looking for his face or someone that could give
a small clue as to what I was looking for, then all of a

sudden it was there; that same scent that lead me to Trey, only this time it did not attract me, it brought forward a feeling of fear and with it anger and rage I fled to the shadows to hide. My body began to sweat with the fear that surrounded me, I glanced to see whom this scent was coming from. My eyes dashed around and over the crowd as, yet I could not see him, but he was getting closer. This fear I felt began to pound in my head and I could feel the need to flee for my safety then in a blink of an eye there he stood with similar looks to Trey, same height and same eyes but it was not him. The pounding in my head was deafening, as I looked on our eyes met, he was looking directly at me as though he was on the hunt, in that instant I awoke with a jolt gasping for air still feeling that haunted this memory.

My black heartbeat fiercely inside my chest stirring the evil that flowed through my veins, I could feel the rage boiling, clawing its way to the surface. It was nightfall hunger tore at my gut it was time to feed. I sprang from my darkened abode and flew through the balcony doors down to the park where I tore into a passing stranger; I stood wiping the blood from my mouth, quickly I looked around then flew back up to my keep. I felt much calmer I could not erase the figure of the man that was in my dream out of my head, his eyes kept coming into focus more than any other detail, it was telling me something maybe a warning, maybe nothing but just someone of the past. I sat for a moment, gazing into the night sky above the city hearing the mortal souls call to me, begging me to come out and play. I arose and dressed to meet Trey. I walked onto the balcony feeling hesitation taking a deep breath I leapt into the night for the city.

I walked through the crowded streets young men everywhere tempting me, teasing me, offering pleasures of all kinds even two or three of them together. Then there he was standing outside of the club looking as fine as ever. I froze for a moment seeing him as the figure in my dream the beating of my heart grew slightly louder, I snapped out of it and approached him. He greeted me with a kiss and we entered the club. His scent was bewitching, enticing, arousing.

" I didn't think you were coming." he said as we walked up to the bar.

" I said I would come; I don't like to disappoint." I said as I studied him feeling weary of whom he might be.

I told him I wouldn't have anything as I had just eaten. He collected his drink and we sat at a table by the dance floor. The music tonight is heavy as so was the air, mystery and seduction filled the room its power overwhelming even I felt a victim of this spell. The air grew hotter and filled with smoke and the music filled my heart as did the ancient evil. I removed the long black leather coat I wore took Trey by the hand and lead him to the dance floor. We made our place in the centre and swayed to the seductive rhythm, the black devil that consumed my soul filled the room with its power and erotic energy. I snaked my way around his body hearing every breath he took, I worked my power of persuasion; people around us became like puppets and every move they made was orchestrated. Trey turned to face me and as he did, he looked into my eyes, I felt captured unable to move just like the dream. He leaned forward placed his lips to mine and started kissing me, it was beautiful, his lips were hot and tender, his tongue wet and sweet his passion intense, his blood was racing hot and the smell of it made me dizzy. I could feel the dark side in me wanting to be set free time seemed to be standing still. I pulled away and looked at him our chests heaved with the thick air around us, a drop of sweat fell from Trey's forehead I caught it in my hand, and as I looked back at him through my brown, I licked the sweat from my hand. Trey took me by the chin and kissed me harder than before and with more ferocious intensity he drew back and whispered to my ear, "Shall we go", then running his tongue over it.

"We shall." Then gently biting his ear carefully not to tear it. I collected my coat Trey finished his drink and we left the club.

Walking back to Trey's apartment the night was rather warm and any breeze that blew felt and in a way arousing. We reached the front door to the apartment this time I could just enter without being invited as once the invitation is there, permission is continued until denied. Trey opened the door and grabbing me by the coat pulling me through the door and kicking it shut. He kissed me as though this was his last day on earth; I could feel my body ache for the sexual pleasures that were coming. He pulled back and looked at me with a devilish half smile then pulled me to his room. The room was dimly lit with a few candles that flickered in the breeze that came through the open window, and the shadows that danced on the wall were in a way hypnotic, and before I knew it my coat and shirt was on the floor. I looked down at Trey he sat on the bed half naked his torso glistening with sweat, I crouched over him running my tongue up his body, he sighed with the feeling it gave, he sat upright with a jerk and started frantically kissing me then rolled me onto my back. He straddled my body gazing down at me running his fingers over and down my chest, down to my jeans and opened the zipper. He moved his way to kneeling on the floor and rolled his tongue around my navel at the same time taking hold of a candle. The moistness of his hot tongue was extremely arousing, he stood and sat on my crotch waving the candle over me some of the wax dripped and landed on my chest the burning was like a needle brief but intense, sweat ran from my brow; Then in a flash the scene had changed. Trey had changed, he now looked like the figure in my dreams from my memory, I felt my existence was about to end; then it was over, it lasted for a moment but felt like forever.

The wax continued to burn my skin the evil in me started to boil and fill my veins with rage as well as the pleasure Trey brought. The bed shook with satanic forces that flowed through me. Trey slowly removed his jeans and then mine, he then placed himself over and onto my hard firm erect manhood. The heat was immense the sweat from our bodies felt like hot rain, animalistic moans came from Trey, muscles tightened through my body as Trey thrusted himself back and forth over me, I could feel my grip tighten around his hips as the deadly razor-sharp claws pierced through my fingertips. The evil was taking control, the windows and walls shook as our savage lust reached climax, the bed raised from the floor still shaking I yelled at the pain from my skin burning from the evil. As we exploded into climax the plastered walls cracked with the forceful energy wave that propelled from my being. The bed fell to the floor and Trey landed beside me on the bed, we both lay there exhausted still the sweat running down our skin. I could not leave yet as he was still conscious. I leaned to my side over him and kissed him, as I did, I drew some of his energy, so he would fall to sleep. Moments later I sat up and he had passed out; I touched his face to admire his beauty and to wonder who he really was. Time was passing I dressed, left a brief message to say I would see him again, left and retreated to my abode.

There were a few hours of night left, so I sat on the balcony breathing in the humid night air and pondered over the visions I encountered and what connection to Trey they had, there was certainly something not quite right as to what I still had to figure that out. I went inside undressed and showered to clean the sweat and other fluids from my body feeling the soothing sensation it gave. Sunrise is getting closer, so I turned off the water and laid in my casket to sleep for my next night of hunting.

Chapter 5

It's been a year since I came to this place and lately it feels as though history is repeating itself. Memories of the past seem to be more consistent especially since I've met Trey. I still cannot figure out why his energy and soul are so familiar but, in some ways, I feel I am getting close. He doesn't seem to speak much of himself, but when I look into his eyes there is something he is hiding, something that I could feel could destroy my existence, his eyes still remind me of those I saw in my dreams some months ago and still to this day continue to haunt me. As I sit on my balcony and ponder these thoughts my deadly hunger pulls at my gut, the urge to feed upon some pathetic mortal excites me and wants more. To hear their bloodied screams delights me with such erotic satisfaction and it keeps me alive. I rise and turn from the balcony and dress to begin my hunt; one cannot dress too fine as one tends to make some mess when hunger hits this hard.

Instead of leaping from the balcony, I decided to behave like a human, as disgusting as that is, and leave through the front door. I stood there for a moment taking in what was around me. The night was pitch black, not many stars and the moon partly covered by clouds. The change in me began to manifest itself the urges grew stronger now just to decide whom to feed upon first. There was a young street walker across the road about nineteen years of age or so, average build; hmm that would make a nice entre'. He took notice of me looking and so stepped up to the curb and opened his shirt, then placing his hand to his crotch and gently rubbed it. He'll do to start with I thought to myself. Keeping eye contact I crossed the street, as I did, he started to slowly walk off to an ally so of course I followed. We walked deep into the ally it was blacker than the night as there was no lighting, I reached the end of the ally only to find he wasn't there; the change in me took hold, the demon came forth. I sprang onto the wall and flipped back over the human; he spun around swinging a steel pipe at me I caught it in the grip of my hand. I flashed my teeth and luminescent green eyes at him then tightening my grip shattered the pipe. He backed away shouting for others to come but no one could hear him, I lunged forward propelling him into the brick wall.

Sliding down the crack wall he fell to the ground taking hold of a chunk of broken timber he sprang to his feet thrusting the splintered wood toward me as I approached him, it was obvious he knew what I was and how I can die there was no way I would die at the hands of this pathetic human. I summoned the satanic forces of the underworld to my aid. The paved ground around us cracked and exploded into dust as the demon forces pushed their way to the surface. I looked around the ally raising any object the lay in my path, solid walls of air hurled the objects at the stupid mortal the dare try to end my existence. He fought the assault I threw at him, he had been trained to fight me, then with one last blast of air his footing was lost, and he smashed into the wall breaking bones in his body. Blood ran from is nose and mouth, he didn't move. In that instant the forces retreated the ally was silent.

I approached the fool and crouched in front of him, he was barely breathing, blood now dripped from his ears. The young man looked up at me through blood filled eyes, smiled and spluttered out.

" Your time is coming; we know who you are; he knows..."

I leaned closer to his face, " Who is He? " I asked then licking the bloody from his chin.

" Do you really think; I'm going to tell you..."

"No. Now what shall I do with you. Should I tear out your heart, so you can watch me eat it as it beats in my hand, or let you drown in your own blood, no, I've got something better for you."

I punctured my wrist with my claw, bloody slowly dripped from the cut, fear and hatred fill the human's eyes as I gripped him around his lower jaw. I pulled open his mouth and let my blood run into his mouth; he struggled to move but it was in vein. The black life of evil was now flowing through his body, perverting his existence.

" Human what do they call you," I enquired looking into his eyes.

" Derrick. What have you done to me?"

" Well; Derrick, you won't feel any pain or fear anything anymore and best of all you'll be forever young. Welcome to my world." I rose to my feet and walked back down the ally.

" Where will I find you?" He yelled.

" My blood is your blood now, you will know."

As I reached the opening of the ally, I could hear his dying screams as he crossed over into the evil slavery that now controlled his new and better existence. I was hungrier than ever I needed a kill and where it came from didn't matter, I needed my strength.

Derrick spoke of a Hunter, a breed of human with the strength of the kin. It is said that many centuries ago one of the kin breaded with a human thus created the Hunter. So now these gifts of strength and training are passed through every generation, they roam the earth in search of the Kin as it is their mission to wipe us from existence. There is only one Hunter, but he has many followers that he trains in the ways of the hunters that have passed. The Kin can usually sense when a Hunter is nearby. It is strange to have come across one of his followers and not sense him.

The aroma of a male caught my attention while walking through the streets, my lips are parched and dry I was desperately needing to feed. A group of young men around twenty to thirty years of age were getting closer the aroma getting stronger. Passing through the group the eldest one took my attention, time felt as though it stood still, we gazed at each other and passed he stopped, then followed me; I had control. I walked further down the street which led to a dark tree filled park that had a poorly lit garderobe, I stopped and turned to look, he still followed I entered and waited. A moment later he came in and walked up to me. I pulled him close; he leaned forward to kiss. I order to keep his blood from spraying onto me I turned him to face away, so his back was in front of me. I jerked his head to the side then plunged my needle point teeth into the veins that covered his throat. It was like drinking from a spring, his blood flowed freely the taste was rich with a slight sweetness to it. I could feel my strength renew itself this one was indeed healthy, I drank till there was no more, he fell to the ground in a lifeless heap of nothing.

I surveyed the beautiful men as I drifted by, their eyes full of excitement as they watched the joes pass hoping they could relieve them of some of their money in exchange for sexual favours. The city was loaded with people of all kinds, shapes, sizes and nationalities, now this was heaven. Music could be heard from every direction, neon lights flashed to catch one's attention in hopes they might wonder in. A light cool breeze flowed through the streets tossing small pieces of paper into the air, I was getting close to the club where I once hunted from when I caught the scent of Trey. I stepped off into a shadow so not to be seen, I watched silently and studied the happenings, he seemed to be alone, but I could feel he was not. A group of five men followed a few paces behind then into a shadowed ally between two clubs, I felt Derricks presence then I saw him as he stepped into sight. Trey walked past him, I was sure Derrick would have taken him, but he didn't, he waited for the five men to pass then at the last moment pounced and dragged the last of the five men into the ally, and as quick as it happened Derrick's kill emerged from the ally. Unscathed brushing what looked like to be dust. Was this human another of the Hunter's soldiers. Trey had entered a club as did the five others my instincts were telling me I was in danger if I stayed but I wasn't about to give in to it. I left the shadows and crossed the street into the ally; I looked around Derrick was dead. With no one around I leapt onto the outside wall of the club and scaled the building to the rooftop as it has several glass skylights, I watched Trey move around the club then make his place in a closed off booth. The five men that followed sat at tables a couple of meters away from him in two different directions. I climbed back down the side of the building and entered the club. It was moderately lit with a mix of male and female mortals, only being of good taste I prefer the male side of the race their blood was full of strength and vigour and always held an exotic taste that was sure to quench any thirsty hunger.

Through the cloud of smoke that hovered throughout the club I could see Trey sitting alone. I examined the crowd as I circled the edges of the room and walked up to the booth where he sat.

" Here alone?" I asked placing my hand upon the table.

He gasped with a fright and answered, " You frightened me, ah, yes I'm alone, please sit down".

" I didn't know you were coming out tonight, you should have said, we could have met somewhere", I said as I leaned back into the chair.

" I hadn't planned on it, just feeling a bit bored you know last minute thing." He explained, placing his hand upon mine, " Are you here long or .... "

" No just thought I would drop in on my way home, saw you as I was about to go passed."

It was dark where we sat not a great deal could be seen, the walls on the booth obstructed the lights from entering which suited me fine Trey leaned forward and gently kissed my lips. His were warm and always tender, he had beautiful full lips pale red in colour. I stood and said I had to leave and would catch up with him later, he said he could hardly wait. I still could not figure out why his soul felt so familiar, it was eating into my brain the mystery that was hidden behind his green eyes and boyish smile. I drifted through the streets with the past few hours playing and replaying on my mind, confusion was taking control and flashes of the past shot up in front of my eyes. Visions of my dreams and encounters with past Hunters; Approaching footsteps from behind echoed down the empty street rebounding from building to building. I raised myself some meters above the footpath and hovered there waiting to see whom this next victim would be, the echo dead-end as they got closer by the sound of them the human was at least eighty to ninety kilograms and around six feet four, this most definitely will make and excellent feast. Then there he was, he stopped directly beneath me. Interesting looking fellow dressed in dark attire full length coat with a hooded jacket worn underneath and the hood pulled up. I descended behind him gently touching the ground and tapping him on the shoulder. As he turned his coat flared open and a twenty-inch blade ejected from the sleeve of his coat. I threw myself backward as the blade whistled past my face. I came upright throwing a punch into his chest pushing him back some feet, he slid through the dust and leaves on the footpath coming to a stop with the sword ready for the next swing. Fierce anger filled the stranger's eyes as he readied himself, I had seen his at the club he was one of the five. He leaped into the air with sword at the ready. With my clawed hands and venomous fangs exposed I summoned the forces of hell, and they flowed through me like an unstoppable forest fire. Screams of the underworld filled the night air as I propelled myself toward the Hunter's apprentice, his sword cut through the air ringing its way as it moved. I blocked it with one arm and grabbed the soldier by the throat and through him into a light pole. We landed to the ground, blood dripped from my arm, and he covered in shattered glass from the streetlight. Again, we sized each other up and he took stance for the ready, now I was getting pissed, my skin was on fired my wound healed and I saw red. He began to charge at me swing his sword in a figure eight slicing the night air as he ran; the forces of evil surrounded me glass and debris was rising from the ground and in the blink of an eye and the speed of a bullet I hurled everything at the assailant.

The debris hit his with such power it threw him across the street and through a bus shelter and the sword out of his reach. It was quiet, so I cautiously approached as I could feel he wasn't done. Out of the darkness the hissing sound of blades came flying out at me, the assassin was hurling knives, I let out a blood curdling roar and spun between the blades as they flew past me some cutting my face as they did. Enough was enough propelling anything I could find trash cans, benches and debris, building momentum, now my skin was on fire my eyes like the hot coals of hell and with one last eruption I levitated the assassin and slamming him into the footpath shattering it where he landed. There he lay his chest heaving with the breath he took, still in a rage I leaned to his face venom dripped from my fangs onto to his face. He let out a gurgled laugh and as he did the black evil manifested fully and I sank my teeth into his face tearing it away and ripping his throat out.

Now I know my existence was in danger two attempts in a week, I know I must find this... Hunter and decipher these dreams, these memories and discover Trey's connection.

Chapter 6

My slumber was uneasy, the battles and conflicting memories seemed never ending in my dreams. Like unto the fog that rolls into a shipping dock details of the past were hidden the torture f this mystery was growing blacker than the evil that already consumed me.

Like the sound of a gunshot, I awoke gasping for my next breath and hearing horses pulling carriages and the whistles of the steamboats at the docks. I opened the doors to my balcony, confusion filled my head, fore I looked out onto gas lit cobblestone streets aligned with manicured hedges and flower beds. Harnessed horses leading adorned open carriages carrying finely dressed couples, men with their top hats and tails and ladies in their silken gowns. Still with some confusion I turned to walk inside, and as I did, I noticed my reflection. I was wearing a nightshirt with lace trim collar, and my hair was longer parted to one side and mutton chop sideburns reaching to the edge of my jaw. I rushed inside my apartment; it looked how it once did one hundred and ninety-eight years ago. Tapestry in the centre of the room, the chase lounge to the edge and a gold ornate clock that sat upon the mantle, it seemed I was back in the early eighteen hundreds. Pains of needing to feed growled inside of me, so I dressed in my finest top hat and tails and set out for the evening's delights.

I strolled down the softly lit street observing small groups of humans exchanging pleasantries as they passed by, so I would dip my hat and continue to the town centre. Hearing singing, laughter, and band music in the saloons, social houses and bordellos meant certainly a different time for pleasures and the underworld lifestyle. I was growing hungrier and the aroma of forbidden lust and carnage was teasing my senses. I walked until I reached the docks where the paddle steamer casino showboat was tethered, nodding to the hired muscle at the gangplank I entered the vessel.

The large room was seductively lit with chandeliers that hung from the rafters, red velvet curtains dressed the huge arch windows, gambling tables were evenly spread so the patrons may easily stumble their way to their next bet. Between each row of table lay a plush red runner that either led you to the bar or the beautifully adorned stage where scantily clad dancing girls would entertain the crowd with their cheeky and alluring movements. Men surrounded most of the tables while women cheered them on, liquor was plenty and flowed like the river. Madams and their prostitutes would weave their way through the crowded room picking pockets and tempting men as they worked their wares and blended into this sordid mix were the Mollie-boys, now my attention was captured. They were the other pleasures of the night; a pleasure a gentleman never spoke of they were like a secret society of the night a forbidden delight.

I made my way to the bar glancing around the room scoping out my feast. I come to seat at the end of the bar not too far from an exit and ordered a whisky. I reached into the inside breast pocket of my coat and retrieved a cigarette case, as i placed a cigarette to my lips a hand reached out with a lit match. As I drew back on the cigarette I looked up through the flame to see a young man in his late twenties. He blew out the match and introduced himself as James. He was clean shaven with black hair that was slick back his eyes brown and lips that were slightly pink and a body fragrance that delighted the scenes.

The bar keeps placed a whisky in front of me and gave a slight nod as he looked at the both of us, I raised my hand slightly motioning for a second drink, one for my companion of the night. I handed James my cigarette, so he may partake, and I watched as he placed it to his lips and gently drew back like it was more precious than air. The smoke drifted from his partial open mouth and danced as it rose between us, his gaze never leaving mine. We drank our whiskies and made our way off the boat.

We walked on a poorly lit cobble path along the riverbank passing the odd human as we went along. I could smell the scent of his blood as it danced on the breeze it was divine and made my mouth water. The stir of darkness in my soul began to rise and the beating of his pule made me dizzy.

The path was now in complete darkness and there was no other being to be seen. We turned off the path into a heavily wooded park where sat a small Belvedere. James led me inside and we gazed at each other for a moment; then in the darkness of the construct James began kissing me at first gently teasing my lips then with full passionate lust. As we kissed, I could feel his heart pound when he leaned against me, and the throbbing in my head from the evil making its way to the surface I so wanted to feed but at the same time wanting more. James's hands crept their way to my waist where he unbuttoned my trousers, his hand slipped inside, and he began to manipulate my manhood, his hand was warm and soft I could feel myself harden and his grip tighten, control was leaving me, possession taking place.

James sucked on my lower lip as he pulled away and gave a sly smile and then knelt before me. Just like the cigarette he gently placed his lips around my manhood and drew back. His tongue was wet, hot, satisfying. I was losing control nearing climax, and the ancient black evil was clawing its way to the surface. The timber railings on the Belvedere began to crack from the supernatural forces surrounding my being. I released myself with a burst of energy that shook the structure, the change forced its way out. My hunger was fierce, my demon was freed, as James stood, he saw my true self. Fear filled his eyes, he stepped back and took a breath to scream but it was too late, I grabbed him by the throat piercing it with my clawed hand. He fell to the floor gasping for air tears ran from his eyes. I knelt beside him and with a demonic growl sank my teeth into his throat drinking him dry. Who needed liquor when the irreverence of blood was beyond intoxicating; my hunger was gone.

As a strange scent filled the air my senses went into overdrive, the whistling of an arrow grazed my cheek as it flew past, I could hear men running. I sprang from the belvedere and leapt into the nearby treetops. A small group of men gathered near the Belvedere beneath me; Hunters now the scent was strong and coming from their leader The Hunter. The cut on my cheek burned and a drop of blood fell as it did, I froze it with a shot of sold air and throwing it aside. The group of hunters surveyed the area for a few moments and then retrieving the body and disappearing into the densely wooded park. Even though The Hunter was gone his scent lingered on, this was surely something I will never forget.

A fresh new evening had fallen, and the ordeal of the previous night not forgotten, and that scent of The Hunter still filled my nostrils, the sun had set for a few hours now and I could hear laughter of young women down on the street as they walked past. I peered through the drapes that hung from the windows in the apartment partially with caution and partially with intrigue, I wondered would I cross paths with the hunters tonight and are they watching me, or do they even know where I am.

As I walked through the dimly lit streets cane in hand and dressed to the nines the human creatures of the night made themselves know to any and all who passed them, some dressed in their finest some with cleavage to show and the painted ladies that showed what they had in order to survive just the night. Such low life did not entice me my carnal urges were of another kind. I walked further along and as I did, I saw black polished carriages stopped to deliver gentlemen to a stately looking house on the next block, this sparked my interest, so I continued to see more.

I come to stand at a long stone path that led to a two-level building with grand oak front doors and two marble pillars to each side. Pencil pines were evenly placed to each side of the front of the building and piano music could be faintly heard coming from inside. I took in hand the door knocker and proceeded to knock twice, the large doors creaked as they opened, and I was greeted by a doorman holding a silver tray with a selection of whiskies and champagne, I took a whisky in hand.

The foyer was a grand room with highly polished floors and carpet runners that lead to a grand staircase and continued to the climb them. Ornate columns rose to the cathedral ceiling where a crystal chandelier hung, iron candelabras were perched at intervals along the walls, rooms to the left and the right where talking and piano playing could be heard, and the smell of men filled the air. This was a Molly House. A place where the gentleman can seek the pleasure of other men of the night. I doorman led me to a room to the right that contains a small bar to one end an array of small card tables and chairs, and several chaise lounges. Large paintings of nude male portraits decorated the walls and gold brocade curtains covered the windows. There were around fifteen or so men in the room smoking, drinking and playing cards and of course several Mollie-boys. Laughter could be heard and the clinking of crystal as the older gentlemen were cheering on the mollies as they danced around to the piano playing and teasing them.

I lit a cigarette and wandered into the next room across the foyer where a large billiard table sat in the middle of the room and had small round tables to each corner. More card playing, and tomfoolery went on in here. Mollie-boys in their twenties hung from the arms of the high society gentlemen here encouraging them to lighten their purses for a more pleasurable evening, some left the room accompanying each other to the second-floor others flaunted themselves in the corners. One Mollie-boy caught my attention he was leaning against the wall next to a palm with a drink in hand. His eyes were deep and bewitching. I walked to him and offered a cigarette, leaning forward he selected it with his mouth picking it up between his ripened lips. I flicked the top of a match with my finger and lit it. He breathed in deep igniting the cigarette and letting the smoke out from his nostrils. My loins began to stir he leaned to my ear and whispered to follow.

The young mortal left the room first; I looked around before leaving and followed. He led the way up the carpeted staircase and down a long hall that had had an open door at the end, we entered the room, and he closed the door behind us. It was a quaint bedroom with dark stained timber walls and tapestries on the floor, only one candelabra to give just enough light to see our bodies. Floor to ceiling windows to the left with red brocade curtains and in the centre of the room a grand empire four poster bed with silk draping from each corner.

The candlelight danced in the young man's eyes as I investigated them, his skin was flawless and smooth. He took my hand and walked me to the bed pulling out his shirt as we did. I placed a hand to the back of his neck and brought him close and began kissing his full lips, the taste of sugar sat upon them making me kiss him even more. We looked deep into each other's eyes not a word was spoken. I unbuttoned his shirt and slowly slid it over is shoulders, his torso was smooth without a blemish or a scar, his nipples erect from the movement of the silk shirt. I licked and bit at them his breath grew heavier, so I lifted and laid him upon the bed, I removed his shoes and unbuttoned his trousers sliding them from his legs and dropping them onto the floor. The soft candlelight gently glowed on the curves of his body highlighting the toned muscles on his legs, his chest and stomach. I removed my clothing dropping them to the floor beside me then climbing on the bed at his feet. The air in the room felt warmer and still. The sound of our pulsing hearts was all that could be heard. I very slowly crawled my way up and over his naked smooth body running my tongue with each advance, small shocks could be felt as our skin touched which made the young mortal's breath catch. I lay upon him covering his whole body with mine feeling as though what beat inside us was one. I licked his lips and kissed him deeply tasting his soul and essence divine ecstasy filled us both small drops of sweat beaded and ran to the dip in my back it felt like hot oil being poured over me.

We rolled over now he covered my body and the sweat on his skin glistened in the soft light. He sat upright and leaned to a bedside table and picked up a small vial of oil and proceeded to pour it over my chest and then down his. After dropping the vile he took my hands and place them onto his body so I may spread the oil over him he then reciprocated. The air crackled with the lustful energy from us and our breathing grew deeper. Once again, he lay upon me then sliding his beautiful body over mine making the oil heat up, he slid his way down to my legs and raised one to his shoulder and ran his tongue up the inside of my thigh, my mind was buzzing, and the blackness was weak. Sweat trickled to the sides of my chest and the bed slightly shook. Moans of excitement and pleasure filled the room as his tongue roamed higher and found its way to my manhood, as he took me, a claw made its way from my finger and tore the bedclothes. He looked up at me and licked his way to my mouth where we kissed like animals in the wild. He then knelt above my rolling his hips over my erect manhood teasing it, teasing me; he took my hands and placed them on his hips and slowly descended onto me. Forces of all kinds rushed through me as he did, he let out a loud sigh as he felt me inside of him. He rocked back and forth sweat ran from his brown and down his body, the satanic forces merged through my body shaking the bed and filling the room, the curtains flapped in the swirls of solid air that was projecting from us, plaster cracked on the ceiling and walls; darkness was taking hold and the evil power that filled my blackened soul pushed its way to the surface, my grip tightened on the humans body we were both close to the explosion of erotic ecstasy. A window began to crack as all forces of the underworld made their presence known; Candlelight flickered and danced across the walls climaxing we both let out a rough scream and a shock wave pulsed from my body shattering the windows and some of the plaster on the walls. With exhaustion the Mollie-boy fell to my side chest heaving for breath barely conscious, my demons subsided, the young man passed out.

Footsteps could be heard coming up the hallway getting closer to the room I was in. I quickly dressed and moved hastily to the windows and as the bedroom door flung open, I leaped into the night leaving the chaos and frantic humans behind. The morning was quickly approaching, and I could feel the sting of the first rays of sunlight, I had spent too long indulging my sexual urges. I pulled the collar of my coat around my face in order to protect it from the sunrise, just a few to go and my skin was burning, steam filtered through my clothes, I threw myself through the doors of my building as the sun filled the morning sky. Exhausted I stumbled my way to my apartment and fell through my door, closed it behind me and crawled my way to my casket and climb in. The black solitude was comforting as it wrapped me in its safety, I passed out drained.

Gasping for air I woke with a feeling of being strangled, feeding was urgent my insides felt like they were tearing apart from not feasting the night before. The evening was moving on, and I needed to replenish my strength, I dressed in whatever was handy and set out to hunt.

I walked through a park that was a few blocks away in hope of a morsel and saw a prostitute and female one at that, in this state anything would do. In the blink of an eye and the speed of the wind I had torn her throat out and was drinking from her. It was moderately satisfying but it was enough to get me on my way.... A scream interrupted my devour and the sound of police whistles rang in the air it seems I was spotted. Replenished I leaded into the night sky into the treetops bounding to each one. The commotion was well in the distance I had reached the docks, now to stalk a real banquet. There were shipping hands, dock workers, men of all kinds. I wiped the last drop of blood from my mouth and walked through the humans at work. I noticed the breeze had changed now coming from a different direction and with it a scent; instantly the blackness in me stirred and claws began to push through my fingertips; it was the scent of The Hunter.

I fled the shadows of an ally to hide, moisture from the humid night air sat on my face, fear of being discovered filled me, my claws grew, and the evil forces boiled inside of me begging to set free. The Hunters scent became stronger he was very close, I retreated further into the shadows, so the light of the streetlamp could not touch me. I glared out to see whom this scent was coming from, yet I could not see him, it was like his scent was on top of me... Then at the opening of the ally there he stood. Tall dressed in black from tip to toe three quarter cape, his face was smooth apart from the sideburns and he had the greenest of eyes that could see into your soul. A glint in his hand caught my eye I then realised it was the tip of a blade, my breath deepened as he looked from under the brim of his hat and turned to face the ally. As he took a step closer, I proceeded to take a step back further into the deep darkness, he was now entering the ally and the blade he carried slid down his arm becoming a sword; my heart pounded harder.

" I know you are in there." The Hunter spoke in a deep husky voice. Then a second blade began to appear down his other arm and two of his soldiers came into sight and they too entered the ally. Fear and rage began to flow through me, and the screams of the underworld filled my ears. I summoned solid walls of air and began pushing it towards The Hunter and his men. The two men began to slide from the force and The Hunters cape flapped around in the gusts of pressured air, but he pushed on. The brick walls to either side of the ally

began to crack from the pressure and particles of brick
flew impacting the three men. The Hunter used his
swords to reflect the pieces of brick away from himself,
so at one last push I brought down part of a wall on top
of the two soldiers only missing their leader by inches.
As I leaped to the top of the building The Hunter
through a sword in my direction narrowly missing my
head and embedding into the brick wall that stood
behind me.

" This Time." He growled at me. " This time."

I bounded from rooftop to rooftop feeling the air rush by
me, going as fast as I could to be out of sight to reach my
domicile where I knew I was unseen. I climbed down the
side of my apartment building and onto my balcony. I
stepped back from the edge and scanned the street
below; I paused for a moment then retreated inside.

Chapter 7

Tossing and turning as I slept wrestling with memories the demons of the past, the Hunter and his soldiers, the scent that followed this formidable enemy. I found myself running through the streets then into parks dodging branches with every step hearing the Hunters soldiers closing in and the Hunters scent filling the air. I came to rest against a large oak tree in the middle of a heavily wooded park; then cutting through the dense night air an arrow pierced through my shoulder shattering my shoulder blade, I let out a grizzly roar of pain, the evil in my soul quickly possessed my body and I ripped the arrow out and continued to run. The Hunter and soldiers were almost upon me, it was then I heard the ringing of a blade and the burning of the steel as it sliced into my back, and with such force throwing me to the ground. Face in the dirt footsteps came up from behind me, blood now ran from my mouth the Hunter had me. He slowly drew the sword from my back making sure the burning pain could be felt throughout my being, and with his foot rolled me over. He looked down at me for a moment, I did my best to focus on his face to identify who this man might be, I coughed up blood and I could feel my demise coming. The Hunter just smiled and then raised the sword and began to thrust it down....

With a demonic scream I unleashed the full power of hell and erupted from my casket anchoring to the wall at the end of my bedroom. In full demon form I looked around; claws embedded in the wall teeth dripping in venom eyes burning with rage. I came to the realisation it was a dream, a nightmare, no a vision. I saw what was to come, I just didn't know when. The fiery rage in me subsided and I came down from the wall, it was evening, and I was growing hungry. Walking over to the balcony doors I looked through the heavy drapes that covered them, just as a caution in case someone was watching everything looked clear. The city lights lit up the night sky and the sounds of traffic echoed across the park and the scent of humans filled the air making the desire to feed grow stronger.

I cut across the park instead of taking my usual rout in order to break routine and lose any prying eyes that may be following. The night air was thick heavy with moisture and low-lying clouds, not a star insight and only the smothered glow of the moon could be seen. There must have been a light fall of rain as the footpath leaving the park glistened in the streetlights. Such a picturesque night for hunting conditions perfect, so dark, so many opportunities. Humans lined the streets waiting to be granted entry in the clubs and hotels beautiful men and of course women, but the men, how intoxicating to smell their blood pumping through their veins fuelled by a night of possibilities. Ironically enough there was club called Sunrise Express. I took a moment to look around the street summoning up the people around before entering. I walked up a flight of stairs to enter the main bar and dance area, multicoloured strobing lights flowed up the walls and attractive men danced in front of them, some tall, some short, some shirtless ad there were those in pairs. The beating music sent a vibration through the walls, and this beat could be felt in my chest. I ordered a drink and sat in a corner watching, waiting for the right mortal specimen to come into view.

A new song began the feeling in the air had changed, it was more seductive, sexual, erotic. The base was deep and hard hitting the rhythm hypnotic the lyrics compelling. I threw down the last of my drink and walked over to the middle of the dance floor and released the black essence of my soul. It swirled around my body working its way up from my feet to my head throbbing in time with each beat of the song. I pushed my essence out into the crowd that danced around me filling them with unbridled lust and sensuality. Mindless zombies they danced snaking their bodies in time with each other; and there he was just the one I was looking for. Hair blacker than the night, eyes bluer than sapphires, olive complexion. His dark jeans looked painted on showing every curve in his thighs and a partially opened shirt just enough to show his taut chest. I pushed my energy out to entrap this Adonis. Like falling into a spider web, he was caught, I began to reel him in. The music intensified dark forces flowed through me filling the club making the humans lose all their inhibitions, the beautiful stranger unaware of his demise. I kissed him as he stood in front of me confusing his mind even more, he kissed back his lips were hot his tongue wet his taste wickedly good. I moved around him my hand on his chest gazing into his eyes keeping him under my spell.

I snaked my body around my subject his hands on my hips pulling me into his body. The pulsing of his blood was loud and screamed out to me. My mouth salivated at the thought of drinking him, the music was changing into another song it was time to lead my feast away. Keeping my trans like hold on this godly looking mortal he followed me from the club we walked for a short while till we came to an abandoned building where I entered, the darkness was comforting. " Come to me." I directed him. He now stood in the middle of the darkened room now was the time. I freed the demon that resided in me and the full force of hell exploded, and I leaped from the darkness, blood sprayed across the floor venom ran from my teeth my claws tore at his body, he tried to scream but as he did I ripped into his throat with my teeth tearing his blood-filled jugular from beneath the skin. Yes, this was indeed satisfying his blood was rich, full bodied and clean, I could feel it flow through me replenishing mine. I drank more of this mortal his warm blood gushed onto my face dripping from my chin, bubbles of breath pushed their way from his throat so with one last intake I once again sank my teeth into his neck and sucked the last drop draining him of life. My cells rejuvenated my skin felt taut I felt alive and satisfied.

An echo in the building caught my attention a demonic growl left my lips, someone else was here, then the sound of a trigger pulling back, it was the sound of a crossbow. With the swiftness of the wind, I hastened out from the abandoned building hearing the whistling sound of the arrow as it was released. Not tonight I thought to myself, but this will not be forgotten that easily now I must be more aware of the Hunters spy's as now I have been made and there will be no end to their hunt.

The sound of my own pulse filled my ears as too the sounds of the city. I could hear every little creek, every footstep as I bounded from rooftop to rooftop blending into the darkest of shadows to escape my assassins. I reached an old cathedral near the park to where I lived, there were two hunters at the edge of the park opposite my building hiding in the shadows. The steeple and the damp attic of this cathedral was now to become my home as I could not return to mine. As I clung to the steeple on the cathedral a cornerstone crumbled in my hand from the rage in me, I let out a growl as I watched the two men below. Morning was making itself know and now I had to find a secure place to rest. I climbed into the leaky roof of the cathedral and started to look around for something to nest in. Old furniture lay scattered throughout, broken glass and other items of ruin, and at the back far corner was a small door, maybe that could be somewhere to rest and retreat from the coming dawn. This was definitely degrading; I crouched down and pushed open the door and behind it found what looked to be an old type of storeroom best of all it had no windows and was dry. I crawled inside and made myself as comfortable as one could there was an old blanket in a corner, so I used it to cover myself while I slumbered.

The sounds of birds caused my body to twitch as I lay there waiting for the night to cover the city, so I may feed and replenish my strength.

The cool night air filtered its way through the cracks in the walls, and I could hear the scurrying of rats as they ran around the cathedral's attic. I crawled out of the small storeroom and walked over to a broken window and looked out on the world beneath me, the brightly lit street, the treetops that swayed in the breeze and the passing cars going to their destinations. I walked over to another window that looked over the rooftops of the nearby buildings. The sound of a falling roof tile caught my attention; two buildings away someone was walking across the roof, I focused a little harder it was a Hunters soldier he stopped and crouched down and just watched the cathedral. I moved back from the window and went to the other side of the attic and looked out from there, again a soldier was watching from that side, moving away from the view of that window I returned to the front window where I saw the park; there were two men in a black van and three more in the park all keeping surveillance on the cathedral. One of the men in the park lit a cigarette and looked directly up at me, his eyes burnt into my soul like he could see right through me.

I backed away from his sight into the shadow of the attic, hunger gnawed at my gut I needed to feed, and time was moving on and somehow, I didn't see a way of fleeing this place. I went from window to window looking for a way out but there was no way the cathedral was surrounded, the weakness of not feeding was getting stronger. I kicked a rat as it ran across my foot and I sat at the bottom at a wall. Some hours had passed and still the men were out there watching and waiting for their moment. The night was moving on, and I was growing weary it was only a few hours till sunrise and still they were out there steadfast in their mission, but I was not giving in to them. I crawled back into the storeroom and covered myself once again with the blanket.

I rolled over and opened an eye to the image of a rat staring at me. I was weak from not feeding, the deafening pounding of my pulse throbbed in my head, in a split second I reached out and fed on the rat. The rodent exploded in my mouth as foul as it was it felt good, I needed more and there was certainly no shortage of the creatures here. I crawled out from the store room weary and still craving, I listened for them as they scurried around, my teeth dripped with the blood of the rat I had eaten and pounced on each one that ran past sinking my teeth into them and feeling their blood explode into my mouth the sensation was wonderful my energy slowly returning but only enough to be sustained a few short hours I needed a mortal, a human a young virile man.

Midnight was approaching I felt strong enough to check out my surroundings through the windows of the cathedral attic, two soldiers still lingered in the park and the two on the roof tops were still crouching by the chimneys on the other buildings. No more waiting, no more hiding I needed to feast. I descended to the next level of the cathedral to find any other possible way out, and there I found a broken window in what looked like a small kitchen, leaning out from it I scanned around to see if it was safe not seeing any of the hunters I leaped from the window landing in an overgrown garden below. I dashed through the vacant lot behind the old cathedral and ran through the darkened allies searching for a kill. A streetwalker, the homeless even a female I didn't care as long as I found sustenance. A rubbish can was knocked over I stopped to inspect it was one of the homeless, a good start for the night. So, I climbed onto the wall and creeped my way above the street urchin, he looked around at the sound of my claws in the brick and as he looked up, I lunged off the wall letting a growl as I drove him into the ground. Ripping his jugular out with my claws and devouring it the warmth of his blood was bewildering and his blood flowed down my chin. I laughed with an evil tone and ripped into his throat with my venom filled teeth like a rabid wild dog tearing apart a rabbit.

Voices and footsteps echoed down the alley it seemed more humans were coming, feeling empowered I scaled the wall once again eagerly waiting for my next feed. There they were two humans wandered down the alley intoxicated stumbling as they went. I thanked the devil and let out a hiss and propelled from the wall shedding the female's throat as I flew past her and pouncing on the guy that accompanied her. The girl tried to scream but the blood just gurgled in her throat, I thrusted my fist into the guys back and pulled his heart out and drank from it while still beating in my bloodied hand, turning to the girl I let out a demonic roar and sprung onto her pushing her into the wall and sinking my teeth into her already bloodied neck and drained her feeble body till she was nothing but a sack of bones. Strength and power began to flow blissfully through me, my cells were regenerating, my hands looked younger the skin no longer sagged on my face I felt anew, alive, reborn.

My hair slick back and wiping the last drop of blood from my mouth I walked out of the alley, everything looked so brilliant and clear. Now some blocks away from the cathedral I made my way into the city, I wanted more, and I was set on getting it and no one was going to get in my way. Men of all types filled the street, music from the nightclubs rang through the air it was good to be back, now to find the main course.

I turned down a side street from the main drag of clubs and at the end of it entered a dark building, this establishment was well known for its pleasure rooms and group gatherings, just perfect to tantalize my taste buds. I walked into the foyer of the establishment reception counter to the right and a reinforced door to the left, the attendant hit a buzzer that was under the counter and the door opened, I entered the dark lit hall then turning into a cloakroom where there were showers and lockers for one's belongings.

After a hot shower I wrapped a towel around myself and went through another door, this led to a maze of corridors lined with the soft glow of red lights, music could be heard from the overhead speakers and the air smelt of cologne. Some doors to rooms were closed some were open. Male mortals walked through the halls some alone and some in pairs all with one thing in common wanting to be satisfied, fulfilled by the guilty pleasures that were on offer in this den of iniquity. Men of all ages, shapes, sizes and nationality roamed here a smorgasbord of delights to be had. I proceeded to a large room at the almost end of a corridor, there were benches against the wall, a good size pool in the centre and steam rose through vents in the floor. Naked men lay on the pools edge as well as bathed in the pool and draped themselves along the benches parading their personal wares for those that desired what was on offer.

A choice of them followed me throughout the room with their eyes, the younger men reached out to touch me as I passed them, I stopped at one very handsome specimen and kissed his steam moistened lips and walked on. The intensity of the sexual tension was electric; after making my rounds in the pool room I left and made my way to one of the open rooms' backup the hall. I dropped my towel beside the bed that was to the back and laid across it. Just moments later I could hear someone enter the room. I took a deep breath as a wet tongue began to slowly slide up my calf, then the sound of another entered the room and the sensation of another wet tongue slid up my other calf. I took a glance down to the two men that were there one in his twenties the other his thirties, and their bodies in the red light had a gentle glow to them. I lay back and rolled over as they continued to run their tongues up my thighs. One gently bit an arse cheek and then my genitals, the other ran his finger over my anus and licked and nibbled his way up the middle of my back. I could feel the strength of their bodies as they pressed against mine, I rolled onto my back.

The one that kissed my back now moved his way to my chest kissing then biting my nipples while the other kissed and licked his way around my manhood up and down from my navel. Then he straddled over my hips and began to motion himself onto me letting his genitals and manhood rub against me. The other human ran his tongue up my neck and onto my lips kissing and tugging at my lower lip as he did so. This was truly indulgent, I released my lustful energy intertwining with theirs the room was heating up, and the air was filled with droplets. The young man lowered himself from my hips working down to my groin while the other raised me up from my shoulders and knelt behind me. His hands crept around my torso, and he pinched at my nipples as the other sat with his legs to either side of me.

I could feel his manhood sliding between my thighs as he pushed himself closer and as he did the friction of our skin encouraged the growth of our appendages, sweat rand from his temples and dripped to his chest. I licked the young mortals neck feeling it pulsing under my tongue, the human from behind me pushed in close sucking on my neck and wrapping his arms around us both we felt as one being. Electricity filled the air sparking as molecules collide with the moisture, the dark forces in me began to stir bringing with it bursts of solid air that engulfed our heated wet bodies. The first young mortal then thrusted himself onto my full hard manhood releasing a moan full sigh, I gently bit at his neck he let out a louder grunt as he pushed himself harder with each motion, our bodies were so wet small sparks could be felt as the friction from our bodies grew wilder the young man yelled out as he released himself and fell backward to the bed. I turned to the other and kissed him as I lay his heaving body onto the bed, I dragged my hands down his sweat covered body onto his well-formed thighs and raised his legs to my shoulders, he began to beg me to take him, I always please. I took hold of his hips and pulled him into my groin and slowly slipped myself inside. His muscles tightened as I pleasured us both, he grasped onto my thighs pulling me in harder, I could see the pulse in his neck throb as the blood pumped through his body. Shockwaves propelled out of my being hitting the walls like a drum being beaten, the sounds of thousands of souls filled my head as the fierce lust surrounded us. The human let out a loud forceful moan and yelled, now we both released ourselves; a screech echoed in the room another wave of energy blasted out and cracked the walls and plaster fell from the ceiling I let out a growl and the room went silent. The two men were out, sleeping, I picked up my towel and left.

After showering I stood outside the establishment feeling the cool night air as it brushed across my face, there was still some revellers out, some drinking, some sleeping in the street and no doubt the hunters soldiers which were still none the wiser as to where I was but time moved on and I needed to retire as this night was fulfilling and very satisfying and much needed, so I set forth to hopefully retreat into my own abode and not the confines of the abandoned cathedral.

Chapter 8

I perched myself on top a building rooftop behind my apartment looking for the two soldiers that held surveillance to either side of my home, I spotted one to the right but the one to the left I could not see. I creeped along the roof to take a closer look and spotted him relieving himself behind a dumpster in the alley. Perfect there was an opening I dropped down from where I watched and bounded onto the fire escape that was on the back of my apartment block. The hunter in the alley turned to look at the sound he heard, I sunk into the shadow on the wall, he shrugged it off and continued. I wrapped my hand around the doorknob on the rear door and gently but firmly twisted it until it broke, relief filled me as the door opened.

I walked down the hallway to the elevator doors that would take me to my apartment, the bell sounded as the lift stopped and as the doors began to open I could hear someone breathing inside, my claws slowly pushed their way out my fingers at the ready; it was a neighbour so I put my hand in my coat pockets and we nodded as we passed each other the doors closed behind me and I sighed, all I wanted to get home.

I eagerly watched the number of the floors light up as the elevator climbed higher then finally stopping on my floor. It felt as though it was taking forever for the doors to open and as they did, I could see my door, what a sight to be seen but still with every sound I heard I cautioned as the soldiers were still outside watching. I opened my door and entered, the feeling of being in my apartment was of relief, the drapes were still drawn so that was a comfort I walked over and peered through a small opening in them, yes, they were still in the park watching and the van still parked opposite. Right now, all I wanted was to rest in the comfort and confines of my casket, the solitude of my sanctuary and best of all, no rats.

The pure silk lining was indeed a comfort the softness of the wadding was so much better than the old blanket and wooden floor of the cathedral attic. I had not slept that poorly for two hundred years and never again. I lay there listening to the wind outside as it blew through the park rustling the leaves and creaking the branches of the trees, in a way it was soothing helping my body to calm and let go. My eyes grew heavy and my body feeling like it was melting as slumber took me over, I fell into a deep sleep.

As I slept emotions of every kind fought inside me, twisting like a snake wrapping itself around its prey. Faces from the past drifted in and out of my mind and began to intertwine with those of the present. The recall of The Hunter from that night on the docks and the familiarity of Trey overlapped, something was coming. Battles continued to play their scenes as though they were on repeat but would stop at a certain point then start all over again like replaying a message on a phone. What small detail was I missing, what clue did I not see, the tornado of visions and emotions spun through my mind and I could feel my body twitch with every motion, then a flash of a blade came down, and I awoke gasping for my breath and holding my neck. I threw open the casket and raised to me feet.

The late afternoon sun was creeping through the narrow splits in the curtains causing my eyes to burn, night had not yet fallen, so I closed the curtains tight and poured myself a whisky. I sipped it for a while pondering the events of the past, present and what could possibly be, and comparing the similarities of The Hunter of the past and The Hunter of present. Could they be one of the same or highly trained and skills passed down to each generation. But if legends were true The Hunter is half kindred, certainly not immortal but ages so much slower than a mortal I think it was time I conducted my own surveillance and The Hunter became the hunted. I returned to my casket and continued my rest till the evening shadows fell, a time when I could roam the streets and begin my hunt.

I let out a deep sigh as I opened my eyes and climbed out of my casket, night had fallen and so I peered out of my curtains looking over the park for it seemed my watchers had moved on. I threw down a shot of whisky and got myself together, not chancing it I left my building through the back alleyway and using the rooftops to make my way to the city, so I may watch the clubs to where Trey, the soldiers and possible The Hunter resides.

I bounded from rooftop to rooftop listening to the conversations of the humans below hoping that there might be something that would give away the Hunters identity but nothing just the usual chatter of everyday life. I reached a building opposite the club to where Trey and the others spend their time. With hawk like vision, I studied every mortal on the street and that entered the club. So far just the usual meat sack, then at that moment a scent; that scent filled the air dancing on the breeze enticing my senses it was The Hunter or was it Trey it was getting hard to tell. I focused harder on the streets below scanning every soul that walked by. A block down from the club a group of five men made their way through the crowded street all in long black coats and in formation something was going on, the scent got stronger as they came nearer. It was coming from the group of men, as I looked on there was one that was dressed differently, he wore a black hooded jacket that was shorter than the others and black pants. The group of men suddenly stopped and the one in the middle looked around, I drew back from the edge of the building to not be seen, as he looked up in my direction he knew I was there watching I still could not see his face the hood he wore was pulled close. He nodded to the others with him, and they continued to the club and entered.

I flew to the rooftop of where they were and watched through the glass dome. It was packed the crowd was thick a mix of male and female humans dancing and drinking, lights flashing, and the beating of the music could be felt through the roof. I stared into the crowd below scrutinizing them to locate the group of soldiers, and he one they seemed to be guarding.

Could this one be The Hunter? I thought to myself. I continued to scan the crowd and there they were, to the back of the club seated in a VIP booth on a mezzanine level that overlooked the whole room. As it was only partially lit the one they guarded sat in the corner and so all I could see was his legs and his soldiers spread around the mezzanine three along the railing at three-meter intervals and the other two either side of the booth. The intrigue was getting hard to resist but resist I must. I walked around the rooftop dome watching and absorbing everything I saw, the comings and goings even the bathroom breaks making sure not to lose sight of anyone. Hours moved on it was now two o'clock in the morning and the group of men began to move. The main mortal placed something on the table and finally came into sight and doing so pulled the hood of his jacket over his head obscuring himself from my vision. All six men came together and like a pack of dogs made their way across the crowded club to the exit leaving into the street from once they came. From the edge of the building I watched as they disappeared down the busy city street and went out of sight. I ran to the back of the roof and leaped to the ground, scanned the back alley and entered the club through the back exit. I walked past the storerooms and stopped at the club doors looking through the small windows in them checking out the club only mortals remained, so I proceeded to go in.

Hot bodies filled the room and the scent of hyped-up men floated in the air teasing me, but I had more important things to take care of, I walked around the room staying close to the walls keeping an eye on everything while making my way to the mezzanine. I unlatched the velvet rope that was the barrier and went up to the VIP booth where the group had been, there was something on the table, I looked around and then picked it up, it was a message, it read.

" Well, my old friend it has been so long since we danced our dance of death. Your scent is as strong as the day our paths crossed all those years ago. By the way how is your shoulder? Does it still hurt? Do you still feel the pain of your shattering bones as my arrow tore into your shoulder? You have never left my sight my dark friend for I know everything, I even know that you are reading this message and yes even your shadow can't hide from me. I felt you watching from above and from across the street, you really think you can hide from me. I merely let you hide. But soon old friend, soon we will be face to face, soon I will end you."

I turned to the mezzanine railing and scrunched the note in my hand and crushed the timber banister in my other hand, my anger began to boil, and my eyes burned from the evil rising in my blood.

" You can't be up here buddy." A voice came from behind.

With claws fully flexed I spun around and with one foul swipe tore the humans throat clean out spraying the wall with their blood; they fell to the floor lifeless. I flicked the blood from my hand and licked my fingers clean and not feeding left this as a message to come for me I dare you.

I walked around to the other side of the mezzanine and descended the stairwell and left the club through the front entrance hopefully teasing the Hunter and his soldiers, daring them to come for me. I took one last look into the street and vaulted into the night sky bounding between buildings to my abode. This night was the beginning to an end it was war and a bloody war it will be, this I promise. I landed on my balcony and peered over my shoulder into the park and snarled knowing I was being watched then entered my apartment and lay in my casket.

As it closed upon me, I went into a trance like state and entered the nether world and communed with all the dark forces, demons, devils and the most unholy spirits, bathing in the rivers of the underworld. Feasting in the torment and tortured souls that reside in this bottomless pit. Screams of sorrow and pain flowed through and around me feeding my soul, fuelling my hatred; pure satanic evil ruled this place and nourished creatures like me. For in this place, I was not alone, my kindred could be reached through the dark entities that come and go. I released my mind into the black fires stocking the flames to burn higher and touch the outer realms summoning others to gather and prepare for what's to come. I could feel my power regenerate, renew and the electricity of this feeling flowed through me, it was like an intense orgasm, my whole body shook, my claws pushed their way through my fingertips, I could feel my skin tear away as the change took place, venom dripped from my teeth as they protruded from my mouth, the pounding of my blood filled my head as it pumped throughout my body, the roar of change shook the underworld with its impact, once again I felt reborn.

Chapter 9

The dusk of a new time had fallen, and I felt anew,
reborn and ready for what comes my way. I raised from
my casket hearing the crack of every joint in my body as
I stretched, the muscles down my back flexed and my
senses were sharpened. I could hear the heartbeat of a
human several blacks away and the flutter of a sparrow's
wings on the far side of the park. My skin buzzed with
surges of restored energy from the nether world,
demons and the angels of hell were at my beckon call,
now, let the hunt begin.

I threw open the drapes to my balcony and stepped out,
the night air was sharp and crisp, and one's breath could
be seen as white mist. I looked out onto the park and the
city lights taking in everything, every bird, every animal,
every rustling leaf and most of all every human
heartbeat. People scurried by like ants on a mission
making their way to the city to lose themselves in the

nightlife and forget their worries and woes. I leaped from the balcony and took flight into the night sky for my playground the busy dance clubs that line the main street.

Standing in the shadows I watched the goings on, limousines arriving with groups of humans, taxis collecting the drunken revellers and laughter that rang down the street. As I stepped into the streetlight my attention was drawn to a figure in an alley across from me, the stranger tipped his hat to me and stepped back into the darkness, he was kindred, my brothers heard my call. We may be territorial and kill any that trespass on our claim but in war we fight as one. My Kin have different tastes and desires, some like me prefer the males of the human race, some prefer the females, and some have both and then there are the feral that feast upon whatever they can find be it diseased or rodent, but they never called to arms as they have not the strength to battle.

I walked down the bustling street listening and watching breathing in the arousing smells of men. Music sounded through open doors to lure anyone that would enter, I felt a sold breeze come up behind me, I looked from the corner of my eye, it was my kindred from the alley his loyalty was strong. A second burst of air was felt to my other side another kin was at my back and others I could sense watched from rooftops and open-air bars along the street. As hard as we tried to blend in with the mortals, we still had a presence, and we dressed to suit the regions we came from. Always in dark attire, I wore my three-quarter coat, the kin to my left wore a full-length coat and a Stetson, and the Kin to my right wore a three-piece suit. Unlike the hunters who only wore black full-length coats to conceal their weapons.

As we walked three became five and we stopped outside the nightclub where the Hunter and his soldiers would frequent. Upon entering the club, the stench of the soldiers filled the air, the five of us glanced to each other then spread out to cover corners of the venue. I could not sense the Hunter his scent was not here. I glided through the crowd watching and studying every human, my kin paying close attention to those that came and went. Through the music and chatter I could hear movement on the mezzanine and feel prying eyes burning into me. I made my way through to the bar, ordered a whisky and sat to the end with clear view of the entrance. My kin and I were only there to observe the hunters, to take tally of their numbers but one false move on their behalf that soldier's life would end.

Time crept on hours drifted by and the tension was thick in the air, the soldiers kept changing their position in the club but to show no temptation my kindred stood their ground and help their place, this stage we held the vantage point we could see every aspect of the room, the entrance and exits and with gestures and our minds we could keep track of what was happening, a mass hysteria was something we wanted to avoid for this war was between the Hunters and the kindred.

A soldier sat to the other end of the bar keeping me in his gaze, I picked up my drink, raised it to him and gave a slight nod, a show of good faith that nothing was to happen here this night and so he returned the gesture. I looked across the crowded club keeping in sight my brothers and the other soldiers as though watching the calm before the storm.

The music in the club pounded and lights flashed, and more people entered filling the dance floor, laughter from different corners could be heard and the fog machine puffed out clouds of smoke into the venue, laser lights performed through the fog as it pulsated to the music and a strobe light set off above the crowd making the humans cheer. My ears twitched as I listened to the different sounds that I filtered through the noise. A low growl from one of my kin as a soldier tormented him in passing, messaged him to keep calm and hold steady. A breaking glass and a scream caught my attention, the soldier at the bar and I stood to attention to see the commotion, it was nothing serious, nothing but a spilt drink and a female getting wet from it. The soldier and I looked at each other and took our seats and to show good faith I ordered him a drink.

The night went on and still no sign of The Hunter, and early hours of the morning were approaching the kindred, and I needed to move on and retire to our places of rest. I gave a nod to the soldier at the bar and began to make my way to the entrance of the club, motioning to my kin that kept watch. We all gathered at the entrance and was about to exit when on a breeze floated the unmistakable scent of The Hunter. All five of us stopped and stepped back from the entrance; then in walked two soldiers and behind them finally The Hunter. He wore his usual jacket with the hoop pulled up over his head, as the three walked past he stopped and turned to me; it was like slow motion as his hands came up and he pulled back the hood revealing himself to me and looking directly into my eyes. It was like everything fell silent our eyes fixed to each other's and like a switch turning off all the noise came back, and he turned and walked on. It was Trey.

It all began to make sense, the familiar scent with Trey and the Hunter and the timing of when the memories and dreams started all when Trey entered my life and his scent was the trigger. I was hard to believe this boy was my age but the Hunter being a half breed his aging process is much slower than that of a mortal. He may not be immortal but still has a very long lifespan.

My kin and I vacated the club and sauntered down the street, acknowledging the other kindred that kept watch yet at every corner was a soldier posted keeping track of our every move just waiting for us to put a step in the wrong direction, one even parted his long coat to reveal the long blade he kept underneath, the brother to my right let out a low growl as to say to back off and the soldier just smirked and flashed his other sword. Tensions were high and the urge for bloodshed flowed around us, but we were not going to give the Hunter and his soldiers the satisfaction of the first strike. My brothers and I came to the entrance of the street, our minds connected, and our thoughts spoke, we gave a nod and as quick as they appeared my two kin went into the night and we all retreated to our places of rest.

I stood on the balcony to my apartment sipping whisky overlooking the parkland pondering my thoughts and the things to come, remembering times that had past and how life was much easier, simpler for my kind. Sure, the Hunter still have soldiers back then and some things were somewhat primitive compared to now but tracking us was more of a task, whereas today in these times the advancement in weaponry and the age of digital tracking almost kept us on tight leash and the soldiers could follow our every move.

A movement in the park shadows caught my attention so I stepped back into the darkness so not to be seen, the sound of a bottle braking as it hit the ground and I could see it was a drunken soul returning from the bright lights of the city. Hmmm what a perfect opportunity for a late snack and I felt I could do with a little pick me up, I put down the glass of whisky and dropped from my balcony to the street below, the human completely unaware and with no one in the street I would not be exposed. The drunken mortal stumbled out of the park and fell onto the footpath so being a concerning fellow I helped him to his feet. I looked around once more and the street was deserted, perfect I thought, and we crossed the street. He was dragging his feet as we walked and mumbling about being lonely and being stood up; to drink this one would do us both a favour. He was vulnerable so i skilfully guided him to a darkened alley nearby and lead him down to the end of it where the light of the moon did not even touch. The drunken fool thought i wanted favours from him, so he fumbled to unbutton my pants. I picked him up by his shirt and put him against the wall, he gave a weary smile as I looked into his eyes. As my teeth protruded from my mouth his eyes widened with terror and his mouth fell open, piss flowed down his leg then I sank my teeth into his throat spraying blood from the torn artery, the blood was warm and satisfying just what was needed for a nightcap. His body convulsed as I drank from him, bubbles of blood came from his mouth, I drew back and let out a demonic growl and went back in and drank from the other side draining every drop, his body went limp so once I had finished, I placed his body in the vacant block behind my building.

The dawn was approaching so it was time to retire. I made my way through the back of the apartment building and entered my abode. Early morning workers could be heard outside on the street, barking dogs in the distance and cars starting. I looked out from my drapes at the motions of humans as they began their rituals for the day and for some tortuous reason I placed my hand into the morning light. Like pouring acid my skin began to smoulder, and blisters started to form, the pain was intense, but it stirred the black evil forces inside of me. As the blisters grew and began to burst a flame exploded from each one and smoke would rise from my hand, I quickly pulled my hand back to the safety of the darkness of my home and proceeded to climb into my casket pulling the lid shut so I may rest and rejuvenate for the things to come.

Chapter 10

Dusk had fallen, and my bones cracked as I stretched and climbed from my casket. I looked around the room and took a whisky from the table and threw it down, always a great way to start the evening adventures. I undressed and went for a shower, the steam was thick and hot clearing my head and the hot water was soothing as it ran down my back, I stood there for a while just soaking it all in letting the muscles in my body relax, a noise caught my attention so I turned the shower off and walked out, there was a bird fussing on the balcony so I went back to my room and dressed.

Ready for the night I set out leaving the building in a humanly manner for something a little different this time I walked around the park keeping an eye out for any misconduct that might happen my way. I could hear the swift motion of breezes in the trees that lined the parks edge, my kindred were gathering and keeping watch. A few humans strolled past one walking a dog and a few in a group heading toward the city. Then I caught a scent, I kept walking looking around as I did and a short distance ahead, I smelt two soldiers on opposite sides the street trying to be inconspicuous and smoking, maybe if they blended in better, they might stand a chance.

I continued past them as though I did not see them, and the sounds of my kin multiplied as more came attending the rooftops and alleys. The two soldiers began to follow me placing their hands inside of their coats, we were just a few blocks from the city, and the tension grew around me as the two soldiers followed. Then with the swift cutting of air one was swept into an alley and all that could be heard was ripping of his throat and the growl of my kin and seconds later the other soldier was carried off his feet and up to a rooftop and he too lost his throat and the dull thud of his landing body could be heard.

Two of my kin joined me as we approached the city the one in the Stetson from the previous night and one from the Asian fraction wearing a traditional blue-black silk trimmed with red at the cuffs. We walked on into the bustling city nightlife keeping alert of our surroundings, the kindred bounded from rooftop to rooftop surveying the street and more of my brothers and sisters mingled with the humans. The army of evil angels was growing, and I was sure The Hunter knew of our every step. Looking around I could see The Hunters soldiers watching from within the crowds and from the balconies of different clubs giving us small glimpses of their weaponry. Posted in every dark entrance to an alley were my kin and to every street corner was a soldier, numbers were growing, another of my kin joined me as I walked through the street making it four, he carried with him a cane that pulled apart into a sword.

Keeping eye contact with my kindred while we weaved our way through the crowded street I noticed the Hunters soldiers were manoeuvring some withdrawing from the balconies above and some stepping back from the revellers outside the clubs, something was happening my senses pricked up and I motioned to my kin to follow those that left and to start spreading out into the clubs, two more of my brothers came to my side the tension was growing fierce war was inevitable.

My company of kin and I entered the club that The Hunter and his soldiers frequent, four of us spread out through the main area, my Asian brother and I headed to the mezzanine. The smell of soldiers was ripe, so my brother Fan and I released the ancient evil surround us and make itself known. Waiting for us at the top of the stair were two soldiers, one stepped back and took a defensive stance releasing two blades from his coat sleeves and the other drew a sword from under his. We both let out a growl, Fan flexed his hands and needle-sharp talons extended from his fingertips and then propelled himself over the soldier with two blades landing behind him. Letting the ancient forces in me take control the air around me cracked with electricity and a solid wall of air catapulted forward throwing the soldier with the sword through the booths. As the other turned to attack my brother, Fan thrusted his talons through the soldier's chest with one hand and with the other slashed into his throat. I turned to the sound of a whistle cutting the air catching a small arrow, and in the same instance spinning and throwing back to its owner embedding it between his eyes, with the force the soldier flew back into the wall. They had crossed the line to attack in a public place of mortals was forbidden, both The Hunter his soldiers and The Kindred lived in secret if either was exposed it would mean mass hysteria and mass extermination, the humans would declare war then all creatures would come to an end. We regrouped and left the club.

Rage filled my being and my kindred felt the same. I looked to the rooftops and signalled, the evil angels scaled the buildings and bounded between buildings that lead them to the abandoned warehouses at the docks, this war needed to be taken away from the humans. Not to bring attention my five brothers and I made our way through the human reveller's blending in to not be seen, our senses remaining on high alert.

I felt a presence in an alley as we passed, there weren't many streetlights as we had almost left the city centre, we stopped and peered into the darkness. A reflection flashed and the sound of cutting air, a spray of short daggers came hurling towards us, we scattered springing off into different directions, some to the rooftop, some hovered and I leaped onto the wall of the alley. A fierce roar was let out I turned to see and one of my kin had a dagger embedded between his eyes. I could control it no longer the black evil boiled its way to the surface I let out a satanic screech and leaped off the wall into the alley. Sparks ignited the darkness as my claws connected with steel and stone, dust fell from the cracking brick walls as I fought then blood curdling scream filled the alley. I emerged to my bothers flicking blood from my hands. I knelt beside my fallen kin as he took his last breaths, a bloodied tear ran from his eye, and I noticed a blade had entered his heart; there was no hope to bring him back and in that instance his body was committed to the breeze and his ashes were swept away. I stood looking to my brothers and all at once let out a deep roar letting others know of the passing.

We turned facing the way to the docks and started toward the abandoned warehouses. Streetlights were becoming few and far between and the night darker as clouds covered the moon. Kindred still flitting over the rooftops and the odd one or two joining us as we walked. A breeze picked up and, on that breeze, danced the scent of The Hunter, still intoxicating and alluring but still needed to end.

Only fragments of moon light now lit up our path ahead as we now entered the docks, the old jetty creaked as the water pushed itself against it, and some of the warehouses rattled from the wind as it rushed through their broken walls and roofs. We entered the old warehouse district and looked around studying every structure. The running of footsteps could be heard from every direction between the buildings and shipping containers. Soldiers scurried around like rats fleeing a sinking ship, and the swift sounds of my kin carried on the wind as they came to join me, some with weapons of knives and long blades and like me some with the powers of the underworld.

The Hunters scent grew stronger as we approached the last warehouse on the furthest dock, there was just one light above the entrance. Two of my brothers pulled open the huge doors and as they did a loud trigger was released, I arched myself back as a ten-foot pike catapulted above me, high pitched screams filled the air as the kin scattered, but the pike impaled three of them propelling them into the side of a broken-down building, one after the other they burst into flames and their ashes collected by the wind.

We scattered to surround the warehouse some to the rooftop covering the sky lights, some to the rear of the building covering any exits and windows and the rest with me. The wind picked up and pitch-black clouds blanketed the moon and rumbles of thunder echoed in the distance. With claws drawn and the vengeful rage pumping through our veins we approached the open warehouse, a deep laughter sounded throughout the building, I motioned to the others to spread out. Two large lights lit up parts of the spacious room, old crates scattered around one end with open office space and winches that hung from the roof and to the other end old run-down boats and corroded fuel barrels. I could feel the presence of the soldiers; then a whistling cut through the still air followed by a gasp. It seemed a boobie trap was triggered and a kindred was decapitated.

A line of soldiers stood at one end all armed with crossbows aimed in our direction, some of my kin growled taking a defensive stance. I stepped forward yelling," Is this the best you've got Hunter?" Then to the other side another line of soldiers appeared holding blades of all sizes and shapes. My kin and I formed a circle with our backs to each other watching every move these mortals. A deep laugh came from the darkness and then there he was, The Hunter emerged with more soldiers by his side, my brothers and sisters hissed as the enemy walked into the light the satanic forces of the underworld flowed through and surrounded us. The other two groups of soldiers moved closer, the electricity of the tension fill the old warehouse.

The Hunter stepped forward and spoke," Still so handsome after all this time, two hundred years I have hunted you, watched you, manipulated your every move, everything leading to this moment in time". He then raised his head and pulled back the hood he wore and revealed himself; it was Trey.

The evil rage filled my body claws extended, venom dripping from my teeth as I roared and the ungodly forces flowing through me. Trey raised his hand from the inside of his coat and firing a handheld crossbow releasing an arrow directly at my heart, quicker than he could blink I caught the arrow and spun round returning the fire embedding the small arrow between the eyes of a soldier the stood beside him.

The ringing sound of swords echoed in the warehouse and the sound of shattering glass as my kin descended through the skylights. Trey shouted the order to charge, and soldiers came from everywhere wielding swords, blades and weapons of all manner. Hellish screams rang out as we attacked the soldiers. Kin sprang into the air mounting soldiers and tearing them apart, blood sprayed from the throats. Swords clashed, and sparks flew, in some instances there were two soldiers on one kin, a blade was driven through the back of a brother while the other took his head with a sword. More Kindred entered the warehouse busting through the rear windows and exits spraying shattered glass as they went.

Soldiers came at me with the weapons they wield but they were no match, myself Fan and Jacob stood side by side, like the other night, and summoned the forces of Hell, sparks filled the space around us, debris that lay on the floor raised up and now became deadly projectiles, using solid masses of air we propelled the debris at the soldiers sending them through the walls of the offices. We three split up and took the assault to the rest of the soldiers.

More of the Hunters soldiers came out of the shadows, arrows and knives came from every direction. Blood flowed and sprayed the walls. A soldier came at me with a sword in each hand, spinning and swinging as he attacked, sparks flew as my claws connected with the blades I jumped back and threw a ball of solid air at him throwing him hard enough to splinter a beam shattering it like a bomb. Kindred and soldiers were falling, I leaped to the overhead rafters to find Trey there was too much to see through, bodies flew in every direction, it was like looking into purgatory. The sound of a slamming door caught my attention, so I ran across the rafters to a nearby window, it was The Hunter and two of his soldiers they were making a run for it.

I took a few steps back then running and throwing myself through the window shattering the pane making it rain shards of glass as I landed outside of the warehouse. The Hunter and his two soldiers stopped and turned to me, The Hunter motioned to one of the soldiers. He came racing toward me drawing two katanas from beneath his coat swinging them in front of himself in a figure eight, he yelled as he lunged for me cutting my fringe as I bent back. With the other katana the soldier sliced at my legs and as he did, so I leaped into the air spinning into a windmill kicking my assailant to the side of his head flipping him onto the ground. I landed in a defensive stance, rain began to fall, and lightning flashed. The soldier flipped himself to his feet and readied his weapons. Once again, he charged, I summoned the dark forces, walls of solid air swirled around me, broken pieces of timber and rusted barrels rose around us; letting out a satanic roar I propelled everything at the soldier and with the impact he was thrown and pinned to the adjacent building impaled by the broken timber. His body went limp as it hung there, his swords fell to the ground and bloody ran from the wounds.

Rain continued to fall, I smelt the wet air in search of the Hunters scent and listened for the footsteps. The wind was strong, and the rain was almost horizontal and there it was, his alluring unmistakable scent the distant echo of his footsteps. I ran through the deepening puddles throwing my coat off, as I rounded the sound of a ringing blade caught me off guard and a dagger sliced through the top of my arm, the warm sensation of blood ran down and dripped from my clawed fingers. I turned, and the second soldier came charging from between two old shipping containers throwing an array of daggers. With my speed I weaved and dogged between them hearing each one cut the air near my ears, then one wrong move my ear was cut I let out a growl grabbed my bloodied ear and firmly stomping my foot into the ground. A shock wave and wall of water rose up from the ground expelling the daggers, steam came from my skin as it burned with fury venom ran from my teeth as hellish screams amplified from my lungs, causing the assailants eardrums to burst. Using the power of the dark demonic netherworld I hurtled all the daggers at the soldier throwing him back into the shadow where he hid.

My ears twitches at the sound of the Hunters footsteps as they hastened, his heartbeat quickened for now he knew he was to face me. The rain was pelting down, and the ground was well covered with water, lightening continued to flash and stick the river, but Trey's scent was still in the air leading me through the deluge.

I came to stop at an alley between two warehouses, lightning blew the dock light, the sound of footsteps stopped; I knew he was nearby I could feel it. I looked around and entered the alley calling for him. My claws pushed even further out from my fingertips, I closed my eyes and turned listening for a sound anything that would give him away but being half kindred, The Hunter had ways of concealing himself. Then the sound of two sharp whispers cut through the air and rain puncturing each shoulder propelling me into the back wall of the alley, they were silver infused arrows deadly to my kind. The burning sensation of these were like acid, I picked myself up and climbed through the broken wall. Gritting my teeth, I pulled each arrow from my shoulders, and on doing so Trey's laughter echoed in the alley.

" Hello lover. I'm going to send you back to the hell you crawled from, you and your... kind will be tombed in the cesspool of shit and piss for all of time". Trey announced from the darkened surrounds.

I let out a loud roar and from the flashes of lightning I could see where he stood. With a flick of his wrist an ancient sword unfolded, it had spurs arching from the blade that caught the light of the lightning. Trey readied himself with sword poised overhead and a steadfast stance. The ground began to tremble as I called on the dark forces of my demon god, I began hurling drums and sheets of iron at Trey but moving with elite speed he cut down every assault that came his way.

The ground beneath us cracked and the walls in the alley shook bricks started to crumble and the rain kept pouring. I looked to the wall near The Hunter and hit it with solid air bringing it down around him and roaring at the strain of the power. I walked over to the rubble and started to dig the bricks away, but to my surprise he wasn't there. I looked around surveying the alley and so as I turned, I was kicked in my chest throwing me through a wall bringing part of the roof down onto me.

Twisted steel beams lay across me, shattered bricks surrounded where I lay and the dust turning to mud as the rain poured in. The sound of the sword rang loud as Trey dragged it along the ground, sparks igniting as it contacted the bitumen. He now stood above me smirking as he raised the sword above his head, a noise had caught his attention for a moment, it was then I took in a deep breath and unleashed full forces of hell with such explosion, the shockwave catapulted The Hunter across the alley and through the walls of the building opposite as well as shattering the debris and blowing out the other walls where I lay. With dark forces swirling around me I levitated a few feet above the rubble, flesh falling away as the demon in me was released, as I descended to the alley I looked around for the half breed Hunter, using my power to clear my path, again, nothing he was a formidable opponent.

I listened carefully for any movement, any sound he might make, sifting through the noise of the rain and thunder for anything. His laughter echoed throughout the half-demolished warehouse I turned at the sound of every direction it came from, rage and fury burning inside me. Then the ringing song of the sword sounded as it unfolded, I turned to face its direction and growled.

The ringing grew louder and like a missile the sword had such impact as it drove into my chest, I was propelled into a wall. The impact was deadly; I was now pinned to the wall and gasping for air. I reached up to pull the sword from my ribs, as I did so Trey came running out of the shadows lunging forward pushing the blade in further. Blood began to trickle from my mouth and air bubbled from my lung I was returning to my human form. Trey looked into my eyes as he pushed the sword in deeper, he leaned into me and kissed my upon my lips and as he did so he twisted the sword triggering its spurs, I felt them tear into my heart and with shock and surprise Trey's widened and he looked down and saw I had ripped out his heart and was holding it in my hand.

As he coughed his last breath left his body and fell to a heap at my feet. The sound of my heart went faint and bloodied tears filled my eyes and ran down my cheek; I could not remove the sword my strength was failing. Memories filled my mind of the evil things I had done and then washed away by the memories of my life when I was mortal, the joys and love I had in a time long passed, a thousand years in the glimpse of an eye. I closed my eyes and let go, the rain stopped, and a breeze blew and as it did, so my body turned to dust and ash and drifted away. I opened my eyes just in time to see my first rays of sun bursting through a broken window a smile came to rest upon my face as it too turned to ash and caught the breeze, forever to dance in god's light.

The End.